LIGHTSHADE

Books by Kathryn Elizabeth Jones
A River of Stones
Parable Series

> Conquering Your Goliaths: A Parable of the Five Stones
>
> Conquering Your Goliaths: Guidebook
>
> The Feast: A Parable of the Ring
>
> The Gift: A Parable of the Key
>
> The Parables of Virginia Bean

Heaven 24/7

> Living in the Light

Marketing Your Book on a Budget
Susan Cramer Mysteries

> Scrambled
>
> Sunny Side-Up
>
> Hard Boiled
>
> Over Easy

Brianne James Mysteries

> Tie Died
>
> Buckled Inn

The Space Adventures of Aaden Prescott

> Light*Shade*
>
> Light*Descending* – Spring 2019
>
> Light*Source* – Fall 2020

LIGHT*SHADE*

The Space Adventures of
Aaden Prescott
Book I

KATHRYN ELIZABETH JONES

Idea Creations Press
www.ideacreationspress.com

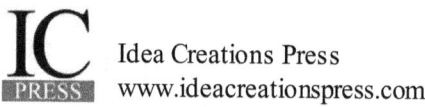

Idea Creations Press
www.ideacreationspress.com

This is a work of fiction. Any resemblance of characters to actual
persons, living or dead, is purely coincidental.

978-1-948804-01-1

Publisher's Catalog-In-Publishing Data

Jones, Kathryn Elizabeth, author
LightShade / Kathryn Elizabeth Jones
First trade paperback original edition. | Salt Lake City: Idea
Creations Press, 2018.
ISBN 978-1-948804-01-1 | LCCN 2018903062
Science Fantasy | Teen-Fiction. | BISAC: YOUNG ADULT
FICTION / Science Fiction / Alien Contact

Printed in the U. S. A

"There is a crack in everything.
That's how the light gets in."
Leonard E. Cohen

To Christian:
The boy who inspired me to
write the story.

Beginning of the End

You'll probably hate me, but I don't care. Most people on Earth hate me already, and if you're reading this book, you are one of the few who escaped. Wait, that can't be right.

But I'm getting ahead of myself.

It all started with the newscast. I don't usually listen to the news, but there it was that day like fire. My mom was making dinner and I was playing with Legos. If you remember how Legos used to be, you'll be surprised that I heard anything, but that day, that day I'll never forget, we were told the horrifying truth.

Mercury was on its way to Earth. Not to visit, if you get my drift, but to crash land. At first, I laughed it off, but then I remembered it wasn't April Fool's Day. It was August 1. It was hotter outside than the heater running, or fire lighting up a swimming pool. If I told you I wasn't scared, I'd be lying.

Mom hadn't heard it. But I blinked at the projected flat screen in shock. Sure enough, the words repeated themselves. "Prepare yourselves," the man said. Like me, he had brown hair on the top of his head, but his hair was engineered fake to look real and was styled in the new ragged cut with curls around the ears. I would have never worn my hair that long even if Mom wanted me to – which she thankfully didn't. He had a frown on his face that was so wide, I knew that if he could be tipped upside down, the smile I'd get would be as big as anyone would give if they'd received what they wanted for Christmas.

Except – this wasn't Christmas. It felt like the stuff I'd learned in Sunday school about the Earth ending and the apocalypse. Except, it wasn't that, or was it?

I dropped the Lego I was holding. It was green. I still remember the color because of what happened next. If you don't believe in little green men, you should. And you should believe in UFOs, patches in the grass in the shape of circles, and the movie ET.

But I'm forgetting already.

My Mom looked at me in shock. "What?" she asked, even though I'd told her the truth as calmly as possible. My hands were shaking, but I hid them in my jean pockets so she wouldn't know the complete truth.

Some things are better for a mom not to know.

So, I told her again.

She laughed.

I got mad.

She laughed harder. And then she looked into my blue eyes. Really looked, you know the way moms do when they think their boy has messed up or told a lie to their brother. I don't have a brother, but I know these things.

She said, "Really, Aaden."

I'd been told about my 'imagination' since the time I knew what people were saying. And I knew something else – something so terrible, that, up until that night and the newscast, I thought it was the most horrifying thing I would ever hear.

"Aaden... really. What fire are you going to start now?"

I'd been told about the meaning of my name for years. Now that I was ten, and tall for my age, I was beyond tired of hearing it. I suppose you want to know what my name means as if you really care, but maybe it will be of some interest to you after you hear what the newscaster told us next. For, after I got Mom to leave the kitchen and come into the living room – which took some effort I can tell you – she stood with her mouth open, as if I'd told her I was going to leave home or something.

But then again, we were all going to have to leave home – and soon – or we'd be scorched.

So, here it is. Two years ago, when I was bored and really had to know the truth for myself, I went to Mom's computer, and put in the spoken password I wasn't supposed to know.

LIGHTSHADE

I shouldn't have been surprised, but I was. "Someone like fire," the computer said.

I looked into my mom's brown eyes, and the television was still blaring the news of Mercury. We had only two weeks to find safety.

Stupid People

Okay, so you're probably thinking, like me, that the news people are the most stupid people on the planet. To think that all the people of the world would need only two weeks to prepare for something as big as Mercury hitting the Earth is beyond insane.

Evidently, there was this big cover-up of scientists and people like that, which had spent years trying to figure out the problem – sort of the biggest math problem you've ever seen. And it finally came to them what to do.

You know those bomb shelters built a long time ago? The strange rooms under the ground where food could be stored, beds could be made, and stuff like that? Some schools even had them once, and people were once building them in their backyards.

I remember some of my history lessons, and I remember Dorothy from 'The Wizard of Oz'. Her family went underground when the tornado came by.

Their house got taken away. If you've seen that movie, you'll know what I mean.

Well, that was the real reason for those shelters. And they've been building those 'bomb' shelters for years without you knowing it, without any of us knowing it.

When I was five or six, I remember having a dream about why we have those bumps in the lawn. "Earthworms," my mom told me over and over, but I never really believed her. If you have those bumps in your lawn you know what I mean. I wouldn't be surprised if there weren't 'bomb' shelters down there too.

I never knew for sure about that last guess, but I knew about the other shelters, and my mom had too. She looked at me with fire in her eyes and told me to get ready for bed.

It was six o'clock.

Dad was home early. He raced into the room, searched it, and, not finding Mom, screamed for her. The noise reminded me of a woman in labor. I knew all about labor, having babies, or thought I did. And even though things like that in the medical field had been eased in 2037, there were still women who liked to do things the old-style way.

Like my mom. With dinner finished, she was gathering plates up and placing them in the dishwasher. We had cooler stuff now, stuff that, I was told, would make past generations sit with their mouths open. But when you're used to gadgets like dish blowers and plants that grow by whispering to them, you're not a bit surprised what people, as a rule, allowed into their backyards.

But more about that later.

Dad came running in after parking the hover car in the car port his blue eyes flashing, and Mom met him just outside the kitchen. She was wearing an apron, wiping her hands on the old black and red checkered thing that had been handed down from her grandmother.

"It's time," Dad said, reaching for her. She fell into his arms weeping.

He stroked her hair.

"Where are the bags?"

"In the airlift; do we really have to?"

My hands trembled, so I placed them in my pockets. (No, I hadn't gotten ready for bed). I hadn't done anything but stare into the living room since the news. You probably would have done the same thing, even if you're eleven.

Mom looked around Dad's chest and straight at me. "You didn't listen," she said.

"About what?"

"Your clothes."

15

"It's six-thirty," I said.

"What clothes?" Dad asked.

"Oh, it doesn't matter now," Mom said. "Not now."

My heart burned. I thought I was going to be sick. It was all over. Already.

Dad placed his hand on Mom's cheek. "Now, you listen," he said. "We have a way out. A place to go. "Rentaurus."

"But they'll never…"

Dad clamped his hand on Mom's mouth. "Remember. You promised."

I stared into Dad's back, wondering what he could mean. I looked over at Mom, seeing part of her face on the other side of Dad's wide chest. He was wearing silver today, like a great ship; anchored to the place we still called Earth.

Dad turned. His eyes were red. He reached his arm out to me. I read the label on the fabric. "*New American*." It was the same label I read every day that Dad returned home from work at *Digitus Flight* (what once had been NASA 20 years ago), but, for some reason, the words actually meant something now.

"Son, grab your bag."

We had packed these bags months ago – it might have even been a year or two – and now, now it was all too real. My legs wouldn't move. I stared at my dad as if there was no tomorrow and felt a small tear dripping down my cheek.

"It's alright, son." He reached for me, and in moments, I was blending in with the two of them, becoming a part of silver and black and red checks.

Crazy Secrets

"Are we going to the bomb shelter?" I asked, shoving my bag into the hover car.

Mom reached for me. "It's time you knew," she said. She looked over at Dad who was wiping his forehead. "Get inside. We'll tell you as we travel."

"Open!" I told the car, and the door lifted.

I got inside, strapped the restrictor belt over my stomach, and watched as Mom and Dad readied themselves for the trip. We could travel far in our Jetta Skyward, even to other countries in a matter of a few hours, and I wondered what bomb shelter my parents had decided on. Though most of them had been 'upgraded' with the latest in technology – a dome barrier between the top of the shelter and the bottom floor of the building – I still didn't feel safe. The news of their locations had been spoken on the rooftops since the word had been given to "prepare" but I didn't feel like doing anything. I was scared.

As the car lifted and we left the car port, we were quickly a part of a sky jam. It was already after hours, but I could see fear in the eyes of everyone we passed. The end of the world had taken hold, and I wasn't sure that I'd be able to hold in my dinner. It sat there like a log and I was as thirsty as a dog without water.

Dad put the car in opt drive and turned his chair to me. Mom did the same. They blinked at me and were silent as if they had no idea what to say. Finally, Dad said, "I know this is frightening, son, but we've been preparing for this day for what…five years?" He looked at Mom and she nodded.

"At *Digitus Flight*, preparations have been underway. Though the end has been coming for longer than that, there wasn't the technology to do what I'm going to share with you now."

"You mean, we're not going to go to one of the bomb shelters?" I gripped the straps of my restrictor belt and held on to the words I knew were coming. Mom and Dad had found a way out, somehow, a way off of this planet, and I would be taking a trip of a lifetime.

"Aaden, I don't want you to be afraid."

"I'm not!"

Mom smiled slightly. "What I mean is, this is going to feel strange to you, and you must listen to every word we say – remember every word. Your life depends on it."

19

Mom sounded just like a television commercial from the olden days, but it was just like Mom, just like her to sound like she was coming from the past. It was the way she liked to live.

"Son, I have been preparing long and hard for this trip. Once we are in Utah –"

"Utah?" I squeaked.

"Yes, Utah." Dad turned his blue eyes to the instrument panel and then back to me. "Once at the underground caverns, you'll need to stick close, not make a sound, and follow us wherever we take you."

"What underground caverns?" I asked.

"Near Ophir Canyon – if we get there."

Now I was truly afraid. "If?" I queried.

Mom leaned in. "We don't have much time," she said, taking my hand. Her hand was moist and I wondered, in that moment, how mine appeared to her. "This has been a secret mission of your father's," she began, looking at my dad briefly and then back at me. He works for *Digitus Flight*, but he also goes out to Utah to work on our craft."

Now I was totally bewildered.

"This craft," Dad broke in, "is almost finished. It's built of the finest metal iron alloy, and the technology is highly advanced – even beyond what you are currently learning in school. The craft will take us to our new home, our new home, son. Do you understand?"

I nodded, though I didn't understand how iron could be light enough to lift off of the ground by itself, let alone with people inside it. "Where is this new home?" I asked. "Is it far?"

"It will take us many years. But the journey will be worth it."

"How many years?" I asked. We'd come far in travel, even space travel. Mars had recently opened up spots on the planet for scientists and math-oriented people, as well as those who liked plants and stuff – horticulture I think it's called. I wondered if we were going there. Unfortunately, we'd heard from Dad multiple times that there was no way in heck that he'd take his family there. Except he didn't ever use the word 'heck.' Dad never explained why he didn't want to venture to the red planet, only that he liked it on Earth and why ruin a good thing? But there was something fishy about how he said it that went far beyond the ugliness of the red planet.

"Two and a half months," Dad said, breaking my thoughts. He looked into my eyes, so deeply I wondered if he could see through my skull and to the other side. "It takes about two and a half months to get to Mars."

Mom's hand held mine tight.

"If you're thinking we're going there," Dad said, "you're going to need to rethink that one. They should have never sent people there, even for work."

My heart stopped. My friend, Bronty, had just traveled to Mars. His dad was an engineer and there were many buildings that needed to be constructed if anyone besides the workers were ever going to live there.

"What will happen to Bronty?" I asked. True fear entered my heart then because it wasn't just about my family escaping into the universe somewhere that now suddenly occupied it. Someone I knew and cared about had gone to Mars, and for what – to die?

"Your friend took a shuttle, right?"

I nodded, though I knew Dad knew the answer. He knew Bronty's father after all.

"He should be out of our atmosphere by now." Dad paled, and Mom let go of my hand. She was as short and thin as some of her favorite plants, still, she held a power I was later to appreciate.

"He hasn't even hypercommed me."

Mom looked at me briefly. "We're almost there," she said.

I looked out the window but I didn't see anything but mountains below me. I was sick inside, sicker than I'd ever been before. "So, tell me about my friend," I asked. I was solid on this question. We could fly to the moon and back for all I cared, but I would find out about my best friend.

"He won't make it," Dad said, wiping his hand through his dark hair.

"Why not?"

22

Mom took my hand again. She squeezed it once – tight. "We wanted to tell you," she said, leaning in to draw me closer. "But we couldn't."

"Tell me what?" I hollered. I was madder than I'd ever been, and heat flew from my eyes to prove it. A slight smell of burning cloth met my nose, and then was gone. My friend was going to die, was that it? He was going to be killed even before he made it back to Earth? And why would he want to do that? He'd have no place to land upon his return!

"What is going to happen to Mars?" I asked, wondering, in that moment how this discussion had started in the first place. Dad hadn't mentioned Mars in the beginning of our conversation. He hadn't mentioned it at all. I'd only thought about it.

"The government should never have allowed it," Dad said, looking into my eyes again. "They've known for years about the possibility. Mercury is not the only planet that might be crashing into Earth," he said. "Because of Mercury's destabilized orbit, Mars might be pulled in. And if the red planet gets too close to the Earth, it will break apart."

"What? I trembled. "So, all of the people on Mars will die too?"

"Yes."

"I have to call my friend!"

"There isn't time. Listen, son; you must listen. You must be quiet and follow every instruction we give you. If we get separated, you must continue to the destination alone. Here is a compass."

Father shoved a metal piece with a glowing face into my hand. "You've been taught how to use these."

I nodded, looking down at the swirling mass in the center which pointed to a previously coordinated point when called upon.

The car had landed. "See the green spot?"

I nodded.

"That's where we're going."

"It says Green-Eyed Monster."

"That's right. It's a cave. That's where we'll find the space plane."

Green-Eyed Monster

I pulled out my best walking shoes and put them on. Now I understood everything. Why Mom had purchased these shoes just last month, replacing the old ones which I'd never worn, that were now obviously too small. Why she'd scrounged through the pack every six months, replacing some things, repacking others. I shoved the compass into the front pocket and zipped it shut.

"Ready?" Dad asked, his tall form reaching a fairly high tree branch.

The place had cooled some since the heat of the afternoon. I wondered for a moment why we hadn't landed closer to the Green-Eyed Monster, but I didn't have long to wonder.

After a mile or two of walking, I could hear cars above me, hovering to who knows where, and then sirens. People were getting pulled over like crazy. In the air, where most of the people drove now, the police still had a time of it. They weren't standing on solid ground and even with their hover shoes on, there were people who thought little of speeding away just before the police officer got to their window. From the news I'd learned that crime had not ceased with new technology, in fact, it had probably increased.

I looked over at Dad. His blue eyes were directing me and Mom to some thick brush. We sat for a moment. "I was afraid of this," Dad said, wiping his brow and reaching inside his pack. He pulled out a water and began to drink. I did the same, followed by Mom.

"What are we going to do?" Mom whimpered. I looked into her brown eyes. I could tell she was tired, and that walking, even in the cooler evening hours, was taking her breath away. Dad reached in for his voice-activated flashlight. "Medium beam," he said, standing. I looked up at the sky.

"Looks like the military is involved, too," I said.

"Yes, son."

"I don't get it. Why wouldn't they want us to get to safety wherever we could find it?"

Mom put her arm around my shoulders. I allowed her to hold me close. "Do you realize what would happen if everyone knew about the hidden space planes?"

"Maybe they already do." Dad took one last gulp of water, pushed on the lid, and placed the water jug back into his bag. "Everyone has been assigned a shelter, one closest to their home, but I've heard talk that some are meeting up with family members who don't live with them – you know, staying together. I guess it's creating quite a bit of pandemonium."

"You know, fear," Mom added as if I didn't know. She took one last gulp and shoved her jug inside. "Ready?"

I wasn't ready for anything, let alone this. What if we were caught by the police, the military? What if, besides the air, they decided to check the ground? What if we didn't make it?

As if reading my thoughts, Mom placed her arm around my shoulders and together we walked with Dad in front of us, his flashlight beaming into the night air. "We'll make it," she said. "Just you wait and see."

The noise of traffic increased overhead as the evening wore on, and then, almost without warning, the whirring stopped.

"Where are we?" I asked.

"No air traffic lanes above," Dad said as if not hearing me. "Over here."

Mom and I followed Dad's beam. It filtered through some rough looking trees and up to the sky.

"We're climbing up that?" I asked.

"Yes, son. We have to traverse the mountain first. Not too far, just a little more than half a mile up."

"How far is that?"

"You need to be quiet. Just follow me."

Dad held back a rope. "Take this," he offered. "Your mother will follow behind you."

27

I reached for the rope, its rough skin burning my fingers and slid into step behind my father. I could hear Mom breathing behind me, and, for a moment, wished I'd taken the end spot. But it was too late.

The journey was worse than any class in school and I suddenly realized that I was falling more than I was moving forward. My hands ached, and my feet burned from stumbling. Every time I fell, Mom would fall with me. I breathed in and out and prayed for her, for me and for Dad.

The skies were a silent reminder that we were in a strange place, a place where even the vehicles overhead were not expected to travel. I wondered when the police would find our car, or the military for that matter, and how soon it would take either of them or both to find us.

"How long?" I breathed but got no answer.

After a time, Dad stopped. "Get some water and we'll continue," he whispered. The rope was suddenly pulled from my fingers and I sat on the jagged limestone. Sitting there, drinking my water, I thought again of my friend, Bronty. Even now he was making his way to Mars. When everything *hit the fan*, as Mom would say, he would still be in space. He'd see Mars falling or something and decide to go elsewhere. But where?

I'd learned plenty about our solar system in science. I knew that with our current technology it took about three years to get to Jupiter. But I also knew that

Jupiter was currently uninhabitable. Where would Bronty and his family go?

Placing my lips against the jug's mouth, I drank deeply. Water had never tasted this good. I pushed the lid back on, and placed the jug back in my bag. Reaching for the jacket I knew Mom had packed, I pulled it around my back, my arms finding the holes and watched as Mom did the same.

"Let's go," Dad said, standing and handing me the piece of rope.

"Why don't I go last," I offered.

"No. You need to be in the middle," Mom said.

"I want to go last."

Dad turned. "Let him go last if he wants to," he said, but Mom wouldn't have it. She pulled the end of the rope. "I'm last," she said. "That's how we planned it."

I had no idea that the planning had gone so far as to include where we would be placed in this mountain climb, but I was suddenly glad that it had been. I kept quiet and followed behind my dad up the mountain. For a time, as I thought and stumbled and got up again, I thought of Mom and Dad and how we'd made it through hard times before, but not anything like this.

Once, when I was five, and before Dad had become an astronaut for *Digitus Flight*, he'd been in flight school and Mom had had to work. Times were tough. She made little money and when Dad came home from classes he'd find Mom crashed out on the couch and me in my room sleeping. I don't remember those times, but I do remember how it was when I was eight and Mom was going to leave him. Dad was an astronaut by then, and he spent most of his time away.

Mom didn't like that. She never told me she was going to leave him, but sometimes, a kid just knows things. When he was home, Mom was silent, and when Dad was gone, Mom would cry. She would wipe her eyes and then fix me dinner, wipe her eyes and then tuck me in. I know she was trying to hide her real feelings. Did she know then that Dad was constructing a space plane for the future? A way to get us out of here when the time came?

I think she must have known it – couldn't have done anything but know it. And now the day had come to leave the planet once and for all.

Dad stopped. He wiped at his forehead. My breathing had become hard. I could hear mom behind me breathing hard too. "We're almost there," he said.

"Dad…" My words were cut short. Suddenly, I stumbled. Tumbling on the rocks I fell down the mountain.

"Aaden!" Mom screamed, as I knocked her down and continued my downward fall. I tried to grasp multiple tree branches and large rocks on the way down, but my fingers always came away empty.

Son!"

Time, for me, in that moment, appeared to slow down. I could see the empty sky above me, feel my breath, the jagged tips of the rocks as they tore through my jeans, and then, suddenly, I stopped. Feeling behind me, it appeared that I'd fallen into a tree. The bark was rough, and the tree trunk narrow. I lay there, breathing in and out, but I could hear nothing but my own heartbeat.

"Mom! Dad?" I called into the darkness.

Nothing. And then, "Aadennn, Aadennnnn, are you there?"

"Yes, Yes," I answered, feeling relieved. But who had called me? It wasn't either of my parents, I was sure of that.

When I awoke, I was still at the tree. It was daylight. "Mom? Dad?" I called.

No one answered, not even the voice I'd heard the night before.

I tried to stand but could not. A shaft of pain shot up my leg all the way to my hip. I looked down. My left arm was lying in a strange twist. "Mom? Dad?" I called out again, before remembering the warnings about listening and about not speaking.

But it was too late for that anyway. I would die here – alone – until Mercury hit the planet or I died of thirst, whichever came first.

You know how you sense things? Things unseen? Well, that's what happened next as I looked for my bag despite the pain. But there was something – someone there, someone who stood watching me. I couldn't see them, couldn't feel their breath on me, and yet I knew I was not alone.

The thing moved. Now it was above me. I don't know when it occurred to me to talk to it, but before I realized what I was doing, I was speaking.

"I'm hurt, can't you see that?" I began.

Silence.

"Where are my parents?"

Silence.

"Is this the Green-Eyed Monster?"

"Yesssss."

If I could have jumped out of my skin I would have. The voice was like tin with a slice of hot sauce. Whatever it was, it breathed out each word as if the very act was difficult, as if he or she were breathing out fire. I knew about fire. I'd burned enough stuff down before this trip up the mountains.

Oh, I never told you?

Well, there was the tree house. I needed a fire to cook hotdogs. And the orchard. I needed a space to sit. And yes, the kitchen. I just wanted to try my hand at bacon.

But you don't need to know that. Not now.

The feeling of someone or something watching me wouldn't leave. As the morning turned to afternoon

– I could feel the heat of the sun hovering above me like some shiny car – I knew I had to change the mind of whatever it was or I would die.

"I will give you what's in my bag," I said. "Everything."

"Everythinggggg?" the tinny voice spoke.

There was silence again and it felt like forever. Whoever it was, whatever thing had found me on the mountain, it was not going to be so easily convinced. I had to think of something else.

"You can have our car," I said.

"Your carrrrr," the thing replied.

"It's at the foot of the mountain. It's yours for my life."

"Your life doesn't mean muchhhhh."

"What do you mean it doesn't mean much! My name is Aaden and I…"

"Your father… to capture him would be something."

"Where is my father?"

"I'm surprised he hasn't come for youuuuu."

I turned my head slightly to the right hoping I would see whatever was speaking to me. A pain larger than the pain in my leg shot down my back. "You've got to help me."

"Whyyyyy?"

"I need to get to the Green-Eyed Monster."

"You are already – here," came the reply.

"I know I'm here," I replied. "Inside."

"Inside, where?"

The long-winded words had ended.

"Inside the cave."

"So, you know where they keep it?"

"The space plane, yes. If you take me to the plane, I will help you."

"Finally?" the voice queried.

I tried to sit up but my strength was gone. Suddenly, something like water reached my lips. "Drink," the voice said.

I drank the cool liquid that must have been warm by now, but somehow none of that mattered. Looking up (I was still on my back), I don't know what I expected to see, but I didn't expect what looked down on me. You may not even believe me after I've told you, but it's still the truth. You know the little green men I spoke about a few pages ago? Well – there he was standing above me looking down. And it had one green eye.

The Cave

"They took your home?"

"Unbelievable as that may be, yes. Why do you think they call it the Green-Eyed Monster?"

The thing sat across from me. I couldn't tell if it was male or female. It had green, lizard-like skin, one eye in the middle of its forehead, and limbs that curved like the branches of a tree. It was less than half my size and wore no clothes.

"I just figured the place was named that because of what was inside. You know the stalactites, stalagmites, and such?"

"I am the 'such,'" replied the green monster.

"You have a name then."

"I don't. Let me see your arm."

I held out my arm and the thing spread what looked like tree sap all the way down it. Suddenly, I could move my hand and the pain was entirely gone. "I've already helped your leg," it said. "Before you woke up, I healed it." It raised its narrow shoulders.

"No kidding." I stood, peering down at it. "Are you a boy or a girl?" I asked.

"I'm neither."

"How can you be neither?"

"I'm sort of like your… ah… pets at home."

I couldn't believe it, not really. My pets, when I'd had them, were loved, they'd all had names, and they were either a boy or a girl depending on their gender.

Still, I didn't think too much about the creature not being a boy or a girl at that time because of the healing that had suddenly taken place. It was amazing to me that I'd been healed by this plant looking monster. Though I couldn't see my parents anywhere, I did have the compass to lead me to the space plane, and I'd soon be able to use the object to find them. Who knew what else this alien plant could do to assist me in that journey?

"What sort of pet are you?" I asked.

"Whatever sort of pet you want." The thing blinked and tried to smile, but it was the most crooked smile I'd ever seen – almost fake.

"Do you have a master?"

"He died in the crash."

"What crash?"

"The crash that brought me to Earth."

"When?"

"Oh, years ago, before you were born."

I thought about my turtle that had died after I'd owned him for one year, and my goldfish that had lasted two weeks. I'd even had a cat once, before the move, and before we found out how allergic I was to him. I couldn't imagine a pet outliving me.

"So, what's your name?"

"Like I told you before, I don't have a name."

"What did your master call you?"

"Slew."

"Slew, then it is."

"But my name isn't Slew," the thing said, blinking its one green eye at me. "I've never had a name."

It was the funniest thing I'd ever heard, never having a name.

"I need to get to the space plane. Maybe my parents are already there," I said.

"I doubt it. If they are alive, why did they leave you here?"

I swallowed. Slew was right. I hated that it was right, but so it was.

"Take me to the plane, and I'll help you find them," Slew said as if guessing my thoughts.

"I only have this compass." I reached my hand into the bag Slew had left at my feet, opened the front zippered pocket, and reached inside. Pulling the compass out, I held it so Slew could see.

"Where do you live?" I asked.

"I live within the trees, taking drinks at the water's edge when I can, but more and more people have found their way here since the beginning. It's getting harder and harder to remain invisible."

"Where is your master?" I asked, imagining some burial ground nearby.

"As I have already told you, he burned up with the crash. His ashes are scattered to the winds." Slew raised its bony arm, and for a moment its thoughts seemed far away. "I lived in the cavern until the men in silver came with their tools, their metals, and machinery. But there was only me, and no way for me to remove them."

Slew blinked once and turned away from me. "But the end is coming. Soon, the space planes will need to be ready. I plan to be on one."

As I made my way to the cave's opening, I gasped.

"No one could get down there!" I thought to myself, surveying the two-foot opening within the jagged limestone. Looking down at my compass the green light glittered. But there was no mistake. I was in the right place.

"I don't want you to worry," Slew said. "We'll find our way."

"A way you haven't discovered," I answered, "after all of this time?"

"You have the compass now," Slew said, "and I might be more of a help to you if you named me."

I blinked, thinking of my parents who were more than likely dead, killed by others who must have been working on the aircraft. If there were others, where were they? I hadn't seen anyone yet, and no one had come for me. What was up?

"Sure. What name would you like?" I asked.

"A good name. One that means something."

I couldn't help it. I thought of my own name. Fire. It had everything to do with fire. "Okay," I began, thinking in my mind of the time I'd found my own name on the computer. There was another name I'd come upon that day, a name that closely connected with fire. What was it?

Ice.

"Neva. What do you think of Neva?" I asked.

"What does Neva mean?" Slew asked.

I tried to remember. It was something about snow, pure snow. It surprised me that the word had come so easily to my mind, the name of someone or something like pure snow. Slew wasn't white but it was definitely pure, at least in some way I couldn't understand. It had to have been pure, at least at some level in order to heal me.

"Pure snow," I said.

"Snow," Slew answered. "I like snow, though it makes me ache some."

"Then Neva it is," I replied, looking even more intently now at the small entryway, wondering how I was going to get in.

"When the miners were here, they found this place – made holes in the ground and went inside. I watched them from the trees and only took shelter inside when they went to their homes. But the next day they would return and I'd find my way to the trees."

I peered closer. What I could see of the two-foot opening resembled a steel wall. And beyond that, the tunnel appeared to slip deeper into the earth.

I was fairly tall for my age, though I had a sneaking suspicion that I could push my way through the space, but Neva was smaller than I was. It should go down.

I turned to tell it, but couldn't see Neva anywhere.

"Neva?" I called out.

No answer.

"Neva?"

I looked up in the trees nearby. "Neva?" I called.

Turning back to the entry I knelt on the ground. Pulling the flashlight from my bag – it was light as a feather – I *spoke* it on. Suddenly, the place was lit up and I could distinctly see the walls. I had been right. The walls appeared to be made of some metal.

Crawling inside the cave, and scraping my hands and sides some as I did so, I immediately felt cooler. I pushed my way back out the opening for a brief moment and put on my jacket, pushed the flashlight in front of me and continued my descent, moving downward. As the space darkened behind me I felt grateful for the flashlight.

For some time, I slithered down the damp tunnel until I reached a precipice of sorts. A huge rock sat before me, and it was hollowed out in a sort of triangle. I slid even closer to the ground, my belly like a snake's, touching the cold earth beneath me. I slithered like this for a shorter time, the beam of my light acting as the eye in front of me, when suddenly the space opened up. I was able to stand for the first time in quite a while.

What I saw amazed me. The wall before me was green and like a large monster's eye. The face of it glowed, and the beam of my flashlight only intensified the glow. I reached out to touch it.

"Don't!" Neva muttered, for suddenly, it was behind me.

"Why not, and anyway, where have you been?" I asked.

"With you."

"Where?"

"With you," Neva answered.

I glared down at the monster. I could step on it in one instant.

"You'd better not," Neva replied.

"What?"

"You have given me a name. I will help you find the plane."

I nodded, figuring it was right. Maybe the creature knew something I didn't.

And then new thoughts occurred to me. What about the men building the plane? Getting it ready to leave Earth? How had they gotten in? Was there a hidden door or something? Why would a space plane be built under the earth? Even if it was built, how would it be able to take off with all the rock walls surrounding it, unless there was an opening for that too?

"Neva, I have a question."

Neva jumped onto my shoulder. I couldn't feel any weight even though I knew it was there. "You love this beautiful place," Neva began. "So did I before the men wouldn't leave it behind. You know, I actually thought they were building it for me. And I actually thought they'd be here. I figured if you came along you could talk to them, get them to release this place back to me."

I looked around, using the flashlight for my eyes, but could see nothing but green, glittering walls. I directed the light to my feet. I was standing in water. There were some rotting steel rails to my right but nothing more.

"Maybe the men got what they wanted," I said, breathing in the wet air that now filled my lungs with heaviness.

"You mean, they're gone?" Neva asked, jumping from my shoulder. I could see the worry in its eye. It blinked once and then again, a small tear running down its green flesh. "Then, my new friend, we are doomed."

I don't know how long it took me to continue forward, but looking down at the compass, I suddenly discovered a new dot – this one was blue – and it was blinking in the direction of the new entryway that had presented itself.

"Look!" I said, pointing the beam to the opening.

"I've seen that hole before," Neva announced. "It leads nowhere."

"Well, I'm going to try it anyway," I said.

I walked a few paces forward, bending down lightly to enter the new tunnel. After a few feet more, the climb went up. I climbed and climbed until I was suddenly in another opening.

"Like I said, nothing," said Neva.

I scoured the walls with my flashlight and proceeded to what I learned was the final climb to the outside world. In minutes or hours, I'm really not sure, we were back on the surface, and I was taking in the heat of a new afternoon.

Sitting on a nearby rock, I reached for my water, some trail mix, and an orange that Mom had packed for me at the last minute. Mom... The thought of her brought tears to my eyes and for the first time, I cried big, blubbering tears until I felt as if I'd never stop.

Neva watched me eat, and it was only after I'd finished that I thought to offer it something.

But Neva only shrugged. "Tree leaves for me. Pine tree Sap. The like. But thank you for offering."

I smiled over at it, wondering what it really was. Not really a pet, not really a person – when was the last time one of my pets had spoken to me in the English language?

I laughed to myself, not really laughing, but feeling the tension of the day falling off my shoulders as I sucked in what might just be my last meal. The juicy goodness of the orange invigorated me, made me feel better, but as I looked over at Neva, watched as it scratched at the ground with its foot, I knew at least one of us was not going to make it.

I'd been fiddling with the compass all morning. It was still blinking that infuriating blue blip. I turned to Neva. It hadn't slept as far as I knew, and I wondered if it ever did. "What do you think of this?" I asked it.

Neva shrugged. "It must mean something, like a name."

"What?" I asked into the increasing darkness. I hadn't turned on my flashlight. Though we no longer used batteries and the flashlight was easy to carry, the life source would dim soon enough if not charged by the sun. Besides, I was feeling depressed.

"A name like you gave me, you gave me a good name."

"So, because I gave you a good name the blip has to mean something?"

"Think of your parents. Would they give you a gift that meant nothing?"

"How did you know my parents gave me this compass? You weren't there."

"Perhaps not, perhaps so."

"Perhaps…so?"

"There is much you don't know about me, Aaden Prescott."

"Hey, how do you know my last name?" I asked, wondering suddenly how he'd known my first.

"Why wouldn't I?"

I wanted to yell at it. Tell it to shut up. Something. But the words wouldn't come. Maybe I should have named Neva after a know-it-all like Einstein.

"I heard that."

"No, you didn't."

"You thought my name should have been Einstein."

I stood. "So, you're telling me that you can heal *and* read my thoughts?"

"And go invisible," Neva said.

"In the beginning, I snuck myself into the room where the plane was being built. I would sneak on a man's shoulder. I would follow him in. And then I would watch – everything. But after a time, they began to see me. It was strange, but it was as if my invisibility no longer worked. They thought I would release the secret, that I would tell them how I did it. I told them I wouldn't, that I just wanted my home back. They didn't believe me. They wanted to kill me."

"And now?"

"It's been a long time since I went invisible for them. And in time, you will see me even when I don't want you to."

"Is that the way it was on your planet?" I asked.

"My planet?" Neva offered. "It was never my planet. Sure, I lived there, but like a cat or a dog or a turtle, the planet was never mine exactly."

"That's sad," I said. "Even my pets were treated with respect."

"They're lucky. I was born for other things."

"What things?"

"Whatever you would have me do."

"I would like you to help me," I said.

"And that's what I'm doing," Neva said.

I looked up at the sky, the same stars looking down at me, and thought again of my parents and their counsel before they'd gone missing. They had told me many, many times to listen, to not speak but to listen. I looked down at the compass, the blue light blinking in the black sky, and at that moment, I knew.

Lights

"We need to return to the cave," I said.

Neva was awake, though it might never have slept.

"Why?" it asked, stretching its limbs.

"It's just a feeling. But let's start at this other side. The side we had to climb up. There's something about it that bothers me."

"The climbing?" Neva asked.

"Besides that," I answered. "Can you shut off the mind reading for a moment?"

Neva stood. "Sure," it said, walking closer to me. The walk was more like two sticks walking, sort of straight and stiff if two sticks could actually walk. I hoped Neva hadn't heard me.

"Listen," I said, pointing to the larger opening that now faced us. "We're going to go in there, climb down, and find that room that appeared to have nothing in it."

"Right."

I strapped the bag onto my back and my jacket around my shoulders, and with the flashlight began my descent. In time, I was back to the spot where we'd stood briefly the day before. Like before, nothing was there, except for a large room with rocky walls and no green gems shining from the surface. I looked down at my feet. No water either, unlike the water in the other room – the green-eyed room. I touched the walls, smoothed my fingers over it until the blue light began beeping as if we were in for some trouble.

Were we? I had no idea. What I knew for sure was that there was something here, something here but unseen, and we were going to find it.

"How long have you been unable to make yourself invisible here?" I asked.

"Oh, I don't know, for a long while now."

"Would you say for at least four years?"

Neva shrugged. "At least that long if not more. When the men began, and before they could see me, I only saw a portion of the plane."

"But I am here now, and the power is returning, is that right?"

Neva nodded.

"Make yourself invisible."

Neva blinked and was gone.

"Are you still here?" I asked.

"Yes," came the reply.

"I know what has happened," I said. "The others, they have stolen some of your power – for themselves. Your light has been taken."

Neva reappeared on my shoulder. Its long legs dangled from my shoulder and I could feel its slight breath in my ear. "How might they have taken it?" it asked.

I looked around me, struggling for an answer, wondering why Neva had asked the question in the first place. Truthfully, I couldn't at first see it, though I knew that it was there. Since Neva's appearance, some pretty strange things had been happening inside me, things that went beyond starting fires with just a thought, words that came to me though I had no idea what they meant. And you have to know something. It sort of frightened me. For some reason I knew if that space plane was there, and I believed it was, it could still be there even if I couldn't see it. And if the plane, men, and if men, maybe even my parents.

I knew, without knowing how I knew, that some of Neva's powers, now returning because of my presence, had been hampered, stolen, by the men in the silver suits.

"What will you do?" Neva asked.

"It's what we'll do," I answered.

I looked down at the compass. Whenever I touched the rock wall, the thing blinked like there was no tomorrow. "Use your power of invisibility," I said.

"All of it?"

"All of it. Now."

Neva shut its eye and the muscles above it ticked in place like an old clock. The wall faded, and a bright light burst through the cave walls, brighter than any light I have seen before or since. It appeared to melt through the crevices of the limestone until water dripped from the stones like rain. And then I saw it. We both saw it, in all its glory.

The structure was large and filled the room to capacity. It was made of some sort of metal, and the surface of it glistened. The compass was beeping erratically now, as if stuck, and I shoved it into my pocket as Neva and I entered.

We saw no one at first, only the space plane, standing brightly against the limestone walls. And then they came, men and women, at least eight.

Neva shuddered behind me.

"So, it's you," a man said, stepping forward. "I didn't think we'd see *you* again."

"This is Neva," I answered. "My name is Aaden."

"Yes, Aaden Prescott. We know."

"How?"

The unspeaking others just blinked over at us, their lips tight. There were six men and two women in the group. I couldn't see my mom or dad.

"Your parents told us."

"Where are they now?" I asked, looking behind the group and around the space plane. I hoped for an answer, an answer that never came.

"You're a pretty smart boy, and that…plant couldn't have hurt you any."

I felt a slight squeeze to my left leg and reached down to pat Neva on the head. I hadn't even touched it before, but I liked the feel of it, all soft and wet like ice cream. After this was all over, I would take Neva with me, and it would be my pet forever.

"Your parents are in safe keeping. We hoped you would leave. But now…"

A woman stepped forward. I wondered if Neva knew the difference between men and women being as it was neither one, but I would have to ask it later. The woman wore silver like the man, and her black hair was brushed tightly away from her face. I thought of my dad at that moment, the label *New American* showing on the sleeve of his silver suit but couldn't feel the same about it now. What were these people doing, and where were my parents?

"I'm sure you have many questions," said the woman. "I know I did in the beginning. Come with me."

I stood planted to the spot, waiting for my parents to step from behind the space plane.

"Please, come," the man said. He reached out his gloved hand. I didn't take it. "If you come – now – no harm will come to your parents."

I lifted Neva to my shoulder and followed her. The plane looked even larger the closer I got, and as I walked beyond it and to the other side, an incredible feeling came over me. I felt as if Neva was healing me from top to bottom, giving me strength.

You have to know something about my parents; they are both as protective as 'heck' – even swear words are off limits. As I was led to the room behind the space plane, I held my breath, wondering what they would say first. Would they blame themselves for not staying closer to me? Would they be tied up like criminals? Would they have their minds stripped of everything they knew and loved – even their knowledge of me?

I closed my eyes, taking in the feeling of strength Neva had given me. When the door clicked, I looked back. The door was shut and the woman in silver was gone. Turning my head, I prepared my heart and mind to see them and I knew, however they looked and whatever they said to me that I would be grateful that I had finally found them.

Opening my eyes, I saw nothing but the other wall.

Neva and I were in an empty room, and we were standing inside it – alone.

"Mom, Dad!" I screamed, but no one answered.

I turned to the metal door and pounded. There was no window, nothing to see out. As I turned my body, I could see no windows in the entire room! We were trapped!

Time must have passed. I sat with Neva and we spoke little. I think it must have known what was coming, so why hadn't it said anything?

I stroked the top of its small head, and the thing crooned like a bird. It was a funny sound, but, in time, it soothed me. I must have fallen asleep because when I awoke, there was a meal in front of me and a pail in the corner – I imagined it was for when I had to do that other thing.

The food was edible but tasteless. It reminded me of one of those frozen dinners from long ago that Mom had told me looked better and bigger on the outside package, though the truth of it was always revealed when one opened it and looked inside.

The government, trying to speak the truth where they once had not, was different now, especially in this regard. No lies – not even when it came to food. Advertising must be completely accurate, the pictures of anything used, entirely truthful. If not, a person could find themselves trapped for eternity within the dark zone of prison.

I thought of the two-week warning of the Earth's destruction, and the lie that had been spread, or the truth that had been withheld until it was too late. Underground shelters wouldn't do it; I was sure of that. People would die, perhaps the people that occupied the entire planet. And all this time a space plane was being built and hidden within the caverns of the Green-Eyed Monster, the biggest lie of all.

No one would be safe on Mars, and the only ones who would escape the destruction would be those who had cleared the Earth's atmosphere. I wondered who that would be, and how they'd be chosen. Surely, there weren't enough hidden space planes on Earth to take everyone away, so how would the decision be made? However it was made, I knew one thing; my parents had obviously not been chosen to be a part of the escape.

"How are you, my friend?" Neva asked. It was lying beside me watching me eat.

"Didn't they bring you anything?" I asked.

Neva was quiet. "No," it said, "but I don't eat daily. You know of camels?"

I nodded my head.

"Camels carry water to prepare for the dry spells. I do the same thing."

"Carry water?"

"No," Neva laughed. "Not exactly. But, like a camel, I carry sap within me for a few days at a time before digestion."

I'd learned about camels in school. "But, you don't carry it up to six months, do you?" I asked.

"Is that how long camels can go without water?" Neva asked.

I nodded.

"I guess then I'm not really like a camel."

I tried not to roll my eyes. Didn't Neva know anything? I looked over my shoulder at the pail behind me.

"No, not for a long time yet."

"Want to try some of this anyway?" I asked, picking up a forkful and shoving it under Neva's nose that was more like two short slits in the middle of its face.

"No thank you."

I took a bite. "I wish I was more like you," I said.

"No, you don't."

I looked over from my fork to see a small tear falling from Neva's eye. "I am not real."

"Sure, you are," I said, dropping the fork on my plate and touching Neva's head. "See, I can feel you."

"But that's only because I allow it. The time will come when you will have taken all of my light and will no longer have use of me."

I blinked and wiped at the tear. It was clear like mine.

"You mean, like the people here? They took your light, your invisibility, and that's why you weren't able to find them. Were they truly invisible to you?"

"I knew they were here, but I could no longer see or feel them. I needed someone like you."

Neva smiled, and this time I took notice. It had no teeth and the empty space that met my eyes swirled in green.

"You see it then?" Neva asked.

I nodded.

"That's good."

The door clicked, and someone stepped inside the room. It was the woman. She brought with her a silver chair and sat down.

"Where are my parents?" I asked.

"Here."

"I don't see them."

"You must be made ready."

I looked into the woman's eyes. They were blue and reminded me of my father.

"Made… ready to see my parents?"

"We are not prepared to take you. Before the Earth explodes, you will need to find your way to the underground shelters like the others."

"Why?"

"Your parents finally understand. We couldn't take everyone, there simply wasn't room…"

"But, my father is an astronaut…"

"He wouldn't leave without your mother. He wouldn't leave without you."

"Mom and I aren't needed?

"Your mother is a housewife, you are just a boy."

"But a boy with skills," I offered. "And my Mom, she can talk to plants."

The woman smiled, but the smile appeared fake to me. It was like she had to smile, had to pretend to care about any of this. I felt the strength of Neva next to me, the feel of its thin fingers on my arm. This was the only thing that was real.

"I can hike in the mountains and not get lost. In school, I was at the... top of my class. I got mostly A's."

"That's good, but not what we're looking for."

My heart sank. "So, where are my parents?" I asked.

"You must be prepared. They may not be as you remember them."

Had it been only a couple of days? How could my parents have changed that much in a couple of days? Still, the thought of someone messing with their brain waves or something suddenly made my heart hurt.

"What's wrong with them?" I asked.

"They have lost the will to live. They need you now more than ever." The woman reached for me but I shrank back. Her hand in mid-air, she replaced it at her side. "You will need to take them with you from this cavern and down the mountain and to your car. You must promise to leave this place and never to return. If you return, there will be consequences."

"What kind of consequences?" A part of me didn't want to know, but I had to know the truth.

The woman in silver stood. She still hadn't told me her name, and if the truth be known, I didn't want to hear it. I'd given Slew a new name, but this woman was far from receiving one, at least from me. "You will forget," she said.

Turning, she left me and Neva, the metal door clicking quickly behind her.

If I told you that the next few hours were the worst in my life I'd ever experienced, perhaps you would believe me. Later that day, after I'd eaten another meal and forced myself to use the pail, I sat with Neva, telling it about my parents.

I told it about my mother, how she used to care for me, and how I used to hate some of it, but I now was wishing for her to care for me again. I told it about our house, school, and the backyard where we grew plants that spoke and ate and sometimes tangled their stems together as they visited with one another. Yes, I know, talking plants were never heard of in the olden days, but the ones in my backyard could practically carry on a conversation – at least that's what my mom said.

Neva laughed. "I've heard about living plants," it said. "What do you think I am?"

"A plant?"

"An advanced plant."

I looked at Neva and took in every piece of it – its three-fingered hands and feet, its thin legs and arms, its one green eye, its non-existent nose and tunnel-like mouth, even its nakedness, and it struck me suddenly that Neva was right. It did look like some advanced plant.

"How did you manage to leave your roots?"

"You mean my parents?"

I laughed then, thinking about the connecting of family generations, sometimes called roots.

"No, I mean, how come you have legs and arms? The plants in our backyard can speak, but they can't leave the dirt."

"I told you. I'm sort of an advanced plant. I come from the Rentaurus System."

"The what?" I asked.

The silver door opened then and I looked up. Standing before me were my parents.

Return

You know how a sheet of paper looks before you write on it? Well, that's the sort of looks I received from my mom and dad when I looked up. They weren't smiling. They saw me; I think. They saw Neva, too, but they didn't say anything – *do* anything.

"Mom! Dad!" I shouted, running to them and hugging them both in turn.

A small hand reached down to touch my hair. "Who are you?" my mom asked.

I looked up at her, tears streaming down my face. "I'm your son!"

"Her son?"

"Yours too!" I screamed, looking over at my dad. He was wearing his silver suit, but it was dirty and soiled in places. Mom was wearing her traveling clothes, what looked like the same outfit she'd put on just two mornings ago – that is, if I was remembering correctly. Without windows, and no one to tell me what day it was, we might have been here a week without me knowing it.

I looked up at my parents. Fresh tears ran down my neck. "I'm your son!"

I thought I was going to die of pain in that second. My parents were there, but not there. Their bodies were the only evidence I could see that they were still alive.

Suddenly, I felt a cold hand on mine. "They will remember," Neva said.

In the next instant, Neva was on my mom's shoulder and then my dad's, pressing his cold hand against their foreheads.

I watched, surprised, as some degree of understanding came to their faces. As Neva worked on them, over and over again, it came to me that they must have been pretty far gone for it to take so long. I hoped the astronauts in silver wouldn't return, at least for a while, and that Neva would be able to get my parents back to normal before they did.

The first real glimpse of understanding came from my mom. "Aaden?" she whispered, falling to the floor at my feet. My dad did the same moments later.

Neva touched my hand before I could speak. "Give them time," it said, collapsing.

I don't know how long I sat there, watching my mom and dad, and little Neva, curled up on the silver floor, but when Neva's eye opened sometime later, we were still alone, and the woman in silver had not returned.

"Aaden," Neva whispered. "Help me up."

Helping the plant up was easy, but its green skin had taken on a yellow glow.

"Are you alright?" I asked.

"We must think quickly. Your parents will be up soon, with a full knowledge of you. But they will be weak, very weak. We may not have time to consult with them about what's happened, but they must act as though the change in them has not occurred. The others, they cannot know."

"That you healed them?"

"As I promised."

"Thank you." I was whispering the words just as the woman in silver entered. She looked down at my parents and smiled slightly. "As you can see, your parents are well, albeit a bit... altered. When they wake, it will be time for you to leave this place. You must come with me."

"Why?" I asked though a deeper part of me knew the answer to her question. Like my parents, they were going to remove my memory and then send me off into the wilderness.

I stood and looked into Neva's eye.

"This thing... will stay with your parents. Its memory cannot be wiped, so it will... be let go of some other way."

"No!" I shrieked without meaning to. I clutched Neva's wet arm and held on tight.

"Look at that. You have feelings for it."

My eyes locked on the woman. "I hate you," I said.

In that instant, Neva released its arm. "You must trust me," it said. "Go with her."

"I can't," I said. "I can't leave my parents; I can't leave *you*."

"But you must."

I looked up. The woman in silver was reaching for me. "It won't hurt," she said, taking my arm and walking me to the door.

As the door opened, I looked back. My dad was moving suddenly, reaching for my mom.

Walking by the space plane, I took special notice of it, telling myself that somehow – at some future point – I would remember enough to do what our family had come here to do. Although stealing had never been on my mind before then, it was now, and as another door opened, this one with windows to open and chairs to sit on, I promised myself that no matter what happened, I would remember this place and I would remember my parents.

I knew Neva had healed my parents and at great expense to itself. It was weak, and I didn't know if it would be able to heal again in the immediate future – if ever. But the words of trust echoed through my mind as I was hooked up to the machine that would take away every thought I'd had.

Only, it wasn't a machine, it was a plant; a plant similar to Neva. It had the same green eye, and blinked at me as it walked, stilt-like, over to my chair.

There were two men in silver in the room – I couldn't see the woman.

The plant sat, and, staring at me, placed its three fingers on my brow line. Closing its eye, I watched as his forehead began to beat like a heart. "I want you to close your eyes," I heard a voice say inside my head. "Close your eyes, and listen to what I have to tell you."

I did as the plant asked, and at that moment, a rush of words filled my mind.

"I am not going to take away your memory like I was forced to do with your parents. I am no longer afraid of them, no longer afraid of myself, but you must trust me. You must pretend that I have. You must play along."

I was about to nod when the plant stopped me.

"Scream, now!" it said.

I screamed, hoping the scream was loud enough, believable enough to convince the others in the room. "Now, I want you to go limp. I will catch you."

I went limp and felt the plants wet hands holding me in. "It is done," it said out loud.

"Good," said a male voice from within the room. "You can go now."

I felt the plant leave, and with my eyes closed, felt myself being dragged. A door clicked open, and I was taken inside and placed on the floor. "We will take you to the drop off point soon," came the voice, this time female. I didn't respond and knew within myself that this is what I needed to do – nothing. When the door clicked shut I opened my eyes.

Mom was leaning above me. "Son," she said, "Oh, Aaden!"

I collapsed in her arms and looked up to see my dad. He had tears in his blue eyes. I had never seen my dad cry. But Neva was gone!

"Mom, Dad, you need to be quiet. Listen… you must listen."

"Where are we?" Dad asked, looking around the room.

"We don't have much time. Do not hug me again," I said, although I realized that the first hug had been my mistake. You must pretend you don't know me. Trust me."

Mom blinked, tears falling from her eyes. "We –"

"So, are we ready to go?"

I looked up to see the same woman with dark hair. None of us spoke.

"Good. Stand now."

I stood, hoping my parents would follow my lead.

They did.

"Now," said the woman in silver, the woman I had grown to hate – even loathe if that's possible – "we will take you to the drop off point. Here's your bag. Everything is in there as before, only you will not need your compass." She smiled.

"What compass?" I asked.

"What is your name?" the woman offered.

"I don't know," I said.

"That's too bad," said the woman, searching the eyes of my parents. "You are the parents of this boy, and we expect you to take care of him."

Mom and Dad looked over at me, their expressions empty.

"Good. In time you will remember each other, but only those portions of your life not in line with what is happening here. We are not criminals."

I stared at the woman in silver and tried not to let my true feelings show.

"Follow me."

I wanted to take my Mom's hand at that moment, tell my Dad how much I loved him and how sorry I was for what had happened, but I couldn't – at least not yet.

We were led out and through the cave. Those who led us, two men in silver suits, took us far beyond the cave and down the mountain-side. I was still weak, and could feel the weakness of my parents who breathed heavily behind me, but I didn't look back and kept my emotions to myself. They did the same.

Amazingly, the car was still where my dad had left it – off the road and near vegetation that would hide it, even from overhead cars.

"This is your car," the man said, "and this is your address. Follow it to your destination. Once you arrive, and before the night is through, memories of your previous life will return to you. Understand?"

My dad nodded but said nothing.

The car was dirty, but as the doors opened at the sound of his voice, I realized that nothing seemed different inside it, nothing appeared to have been removed since our landing.

Dad started the car and we took off, leaving the place we thought would lead to safety and up again to home.

Time Moves

Arriving at the car port, dad landed the hover car and we walked inside. The place, like the inside of our car, was just as we'd left it.

Mom turned to me and smiled. Holding her arms out, I ran to her, bawling like a newborn baby. Dad reached in and held us all close. We stood that way in our living room for a while, still not speaking, still not trusting the freedom that we'd been given. And then it came:

"Son, we prayed that you'd be alright."

"Aaden, how did you find us? How did you know where we were?"

"The compass?"

"But how did you see us? The shield was up..." Dad began.

"That would have to be Neva."

"Neva?" Mom asked, squeezing me one last time as we walked to the couch.

"The plant."

"Slew?" Mom asked.

"No, not Slew. The one *I* know. The plant that was with me was of the perennial Slew type. I gave it a name. Now it's Neva."

"Maybe they're all known as Slew before someone names them – if they name them at all," Mom said.

"That makes sense," said Dad, who slid his large form so close to me I felt like the inside of a sandwich between them.

"Even when the plant was taking away our thoughts it was speaking to us, telling us that it wouldn't be for long. Of course, I didn't remember this until later, but by then, you had been taken from the room."

"That's when your… Slew talked to me," I said. "It told me that I was to pretend not to know anything, so I just went along with it, hoping I was doing the right thing."

Mom hugged me again, sideways, as we sat on the couch together.

"Once we were discovered on the mountain," Dad began, "Mom and I got to work trying to figure out how we'd find you and get on that plane."

"Unfortunately, our plans were cut short with the erasing of our memory," Mom added wearily. She looked so tired, even more tired than at the end of the day when she'd cook Dad and me dinner and finally have time to relax.

"When I woke up on the mountain to find that you and Dad were gone, I found this plant – or you could say Neva found me, and it, along with the beeping compass, helped me find the space plane. With the help of its powers of invisibility I was able to find the hidden place where you and Dad were."

"That's crazy," Dad said. "The compass has no real power; though you must have done something right because we're all here." He reached for me, placing his thick arm around my small shoulders. "I'm sorry, son. I should have told you about the Green-Eyed Monster."

"But Mom knew," I ventured.

"No, not at first." Dad looked briefly at Mom and touched her arm. "Until a few days ago when I rushed home to tell you and Mom to get your bags, I had been told we'd be able to leave with the few others who'd been chosen to take flight based on our special skills, but it was only after we had ascended the mountain and were taken that I discovered the terrible truth."

"I was there, just where you'd left me," I said, thinking of it now and how lonely I'd been before Neva had found me.

"We were taken just as we reached the crest of the hill. Looking back, we didn't see you."

I thought about Neva and answered: "Neva has some interesting gifts, invisibility for one. It can also heal. But Neva is all about speaking the truth too – and doing it."

"That's what Slew told us before it took away our memory. It said it had to follow through with what its master said."

"Even if it wasn't right?" I asked.

Mom nodded, caressing my hand.

"But that doesn't make sense. Your same Slew didn't take away my memory but lied that it had."

This time Dad shrugged. "Maybe it doesn't matter," he said. "What does is that we get back to the Green-Eyed Monster before it's too late."

I didn't sleep well that night, but Mom and Dad said they needed the evening to get things put together. All I could think about was Neva. What if it was dead? I wondered how we were going to get back to the cavern before the Earth exploded without being seen. I wondered about the noise coming from my bedroom window. Since our return, all I could hear was howling in the distance, like great crying without ceasing. Dogs barked all night, and some of the homes had been emptied, their hover cars gone from their car ports. Many people had already left for the underground shelters and garbage covered the walk. Words in neon blinked on hover billboards: *Find a shelter near you. Don't be left in the dust. The time is at hand to safeguard your family.*

The words made me sick, and they all came back to me now as I lay in bed thinking about our return drive home. I thought about my friend again, Bronty, on his way to Mars. He hadn't landed yet; it would be some time before he did if the planet didn't turn out of orbit, that is. I didn't want him to die just like I didn't want my mom and dad to die, Neva to die. How could I save them all – including myself?

I must have slept. When I opened my eyes, I couldn't even hear the birds, though my parents were already in my room.

"We've packed this," Dad said, holding out the colored bag as if it was nothing but cloth-covered air. "Everything is in there except a compass."

"Sorry about that." Mom looked down on me and stroked my hair like she would a puppy. But we hadn't had a puppy for a long time, and I doubted we would ever again.

"I have a compass. We had an extra one in the airlift. Now listen, son, we're going to have to make this trip on foot."

"Again?" I sat up straight in bed.

"Get your clothes on. You'll need to wear long pants. Wear your hiking boots. Got it?"

I nodded.

"Here's a hat," Mom said, handing me a Falcon hat with a yellow and blue stripe across its bill. "We should have thought this through the first time."

I put the thing on, even though I was still in my clothes from the past week. Mom hadn't even asked me to take a shower, and it didn't look like she was going to ask me to take one now.

"A shower?" I asked, hoping some normal stuff would somehow come creeping back into my life even if I hated it.

"If you want," Mom said, "but make it quick."

Mom had never been quick about anything in her life. It was all about the old ways, taking the air in and blowing it out slowly, taking care of the plants out back, speaking to them in a soft voice so they wouldn't be afraid, stuff like that.

I decided to take a shower and did so quickly.

Sliding on my clothes, I returned from the bathroom only to find my parents waiting for me. "Do you have everything?" Mom asked.

I nodded.

"We'll take the hover car to the nearest shelter, drop it off close by, and leave from there."

"Why?" I asked.

"If those people are monitoring us in any way, they will think we've done like the others; gone to the nearest shelter for safety."

A sudden thought made my heart sink. "But what if they…"

My dad stopped me with his hand. "That's already been checked. They have no listening or viewing devices, which surprised me, I can tell you."

"When did you check?"

"Last night."

"When did you sleep?" I asked. It was then I realized that Dad hadn't slept. I looked into his blue eyes. They were red around the white part and there were dark shadows underneath his eyes. Mom's eyes looked better, but not by much.

We left the house and entered the car port on the roof. "Open!" I said to the car and got in, and just like a little over a week ago, my Dad started the car with the sound of his voice and with a *whirr* of the anti-gravity engine, we were off to the shelter.

I don't know if you'll believe me when I tell you what happened next, but it was sort of eerie; you know? There were very few people on the roads. Dogs and cats roamed the roads without their owners because animals hadn't been allowed into the shelters.

I thought briefly of Neva, and then turned my attention back to the sky. Our shelter was one that had been built under my elementary school. I'd always thought it funny that during the years of advancements, the place had never been destroyed. *We didn't need it now*, I'd thought then. But now I knew the truth. The shelters weren't just shelters now. They were insulated with a thick dome barrier. I looked down at the ground as we landed in a spot about three blocks from my school. All I could see was trash, stray dogs, and a few people walking the streets. *The homeless*, I thought but didn't say. These, I'd learned from my parents who had watched the news even as I dreamt of saving those I loved, wouldn't have a shelter to go in to. There were no shelters for the homeless where disease could be spread to others.

I felt sorry for the homeless, though I knew more and more of them were taking up residence inside the once protective above-ground domes. Still, they would die like the others who believed they would be safe below ground.

"Make sure you have your bag," Mom reminded me, though it was the last thing I would forget. I grabbed the thing by the straps and got out of the car. "Close," I said, though I doubted even locking the car tight would matter now.

Mom smiled wearily at me, placing her own colored bag around her shoulders. Dad took out the compass. He was still wearing his silver suit, not trading it in for regular clothes like the rest of us. "Begin," he said. He looked over at me as the compass lit up. The dot was green but quickly turned to blue as Dad spoke to it.

"It's your turn," Dad said, looking at me.

"For what?" I answered. I looked around. There was a police car just a few feet up from us – military personnel standing just a few feet away.

"You need to whisper, son," Dad said, touching my arm. "It's time."

Was I missing something? I looked up at Mom. "It's okay," she said, smiling as if she was merely looking at her garden of flowers. I hadn't even said goodbye to them but I'm sure she had. And then I knew.

I touched the compass and closed my eyes, reminding myself of the way I felt inside the cave when the walls had dissolved and I'd seen the space plane for the first time.

Invisibility

I followed Mom and Dad through the brush and away from the imaginary safety of the shelter, hoping that it had worked. We passed one soldier and then two, a police car nearer the fence that led to the cavern, and finally, the water and the men positioned there. I knew we were invisible.

I was grateful we were invisible to others; though I wasn't sure if I should speak.

Mom placed her fingers to her lips – my answer. As we walked along, for miles it seemed, watching families enter shelters, the homeless finding a dome to stay in, watching the dogs and cats search for food, hearing the plants crying in backyards for their owners (my mom said she could hear them), how lucky me and my family were.

We had a space plane, while many on the Earth would be destroyed.

Still, I wondered how many space planes had been built in the five-year period when technology had obviously been great enough to think beyond Earthly domes and underground shelters. How many people would survive? And who had the government chosen to save?

And then something else struck me.

How did Mom and Dad know about my gift of invisibility, when I hadn't really thought about it until now?

I couldn't ask them, at least not yet. All I could do was follow behind my dad, feeling the breath of my mom behind me.

At the base of the mountain, Dad turned to me and we stopped.

"That was good, son," he said. "How are you feeling?"

"Good," I said, "but why didn't you tell me?"

Dad hesitated for only a minute. "We didn't want you to worry. We knew of your power because you told us. Mom and I are very grateful."

"Do you think they've killed Neva?" I asked.

I took the rope that Dad handed me, and gave the remainder to Mom.

"Perhaps," Dad said, though their physiology is quite a bit different from our own. They would have had to know how to do that."

"That's right," I said, my feet brushing against the rocks as we climbed. I listened for Mom from behind me; I wanted to make sure she was alright.

At the top of the mountain, Dad held up his hand. "Are we still invisible?" he asked me. Without anyone around us, it wasn't easy to see truth, though the compass' blue light was still blinking in the direction of the space plane.

"How many of them are there?" I asked now, standing on the ledge trying not to look down on the world we'd come from.

"How many what?"

"Space planes."

"Only one here; about twenty others scattered throughout the world. But we must be quiet…"

Dad pushed the thick rope inside his bag and zipped it closed.

I wanted to ask Dad how many people could fit inside a plane, where we were going, how long it would take to get there and so on, but I listened instead. Listening had gotten all of us this far, and I didn't want to ruin anything.

At the cave's opening, Dad turned off the compass and slid it into the bag's front pocket. I slid on my belly behind him with Mom behind me, making the same progress I'd made recently – fortunately, under very different conditions.

I stopped once and tried to look back at Mom. What I saw mostly was blackness. Occasionally Dad would light up the area with his flashlight, but only briefly. Then, once again we'd be in darkness. As before, the cave was wet, a bit slimy, and as we slid through the small precipice to the Green-Eyed Monster, Mom gasped.

I had seen it too, lying motionless near the opening – Neva.

I knew Neva needed pine tree sap to keep it going, but I hadn't thought to bring any. I felt foolish about that, so terrible I wouldn't look at it at first. Anyway, Neva was more than likely dead.

I touched its skin, revealing myself to it so that it would know I was there. Neva's eye was closed and its skin yellower than when I'd last seen it.

"Neva?" I asked, checking for a heartbeat, but there was nothing. Still, I had no idea where its heart would be located if, indeed it had one. But it had to have one.

"Closer to the stomach," Dad said, reaching inside his bag for something. I placed my hand on Neva's stomach and discovered a faint beating noise. "Neva's alive," I said.

"Give it some of this," Dad answered, handing me a fresh tree branch about the width of my forefinger. Sap oozed from the bark. I pushed my finger into the sap and placed the sap at Neva's mouth. A large, purple tongue reached out, taking the sap like a shovel.

I would be lying to you if I told you I didn't jump. All this time I'd thought the mouth of Neva was

81

only hollow and green, but I couldn't believe that anymore. I brushed more tree sap on the tongue, watching it go into the depths of the green mouth and then push out for more. I continued this process until the sap was gone.

I handed the branch back to Dad. "I hope this works," I said, though I wondered mightily if it would. How had my dad known to get the tree branch anyway? How had he known about the sap? How had he learned about Neva's heart?

I didn't have time to ask, at least not yet. Neva was opening its eye, the yellowish sheen suddenly turning to a glimmering green. I watched its skin change right before my eyes, and heard it speak: "Aaden, my friend, is that really youuuuu?"

Moments later, we were moving through the cave; Neva perched on my shoulder once we'd slid our bellies through the narrowest point of the tunnel. At the other end, we stood, all invisible, watching the space plane in all its glory.

Something was happening today, something different. As the craft hummed, there was movement nearby, almost as if everyone was lining up to get into the craft, but I couldn't see anyone. Moments later, the humming ended; a few astronauts in silver descended the stairs and made their way into the second room with the windows.

We all watched as they gathered; even though we couldn't hear their words, something was happening that we couldn't mistake.

"Slew is in there. It is speaking to me even now."

I heard Neva's voice speaking into my thoughts and wondered if my parents could hear it. Seconds later, I knew they couldn't. "Tell your parents that the time has almost arrived. Tomorrow morning the others will be coming."

"What others?" I asked Neva.

"Those in the government and doctors."

I turned to my dad. "Neva says they are coming. The government – doctors."

Dad blinked over at me and then at the door.

"We need to be careful. Though invisible, they will still be able to hear us."

Dad nodded. Mom grabbed my hand. Neva slid off my shoulder.

"Neva says: Slew is aware of our presence. It will help us to remain hidden."

Dad nodded.

"We must go into the second room. Now!"

Dad took Mom's hand and Neva took mine. We tiptoed without incident into the second room and shut the door behind us.

"They will not look in here, at least for some time," Neva offered, this time out loud. "They are more interested in bringing in the others, getting them ready for the journey."

"Who will be coming?" Dad asked.

"Like you've already heard. Government officials, doctors, people of money and prominence."

Mom rolled her eyes. "And women?"

"What is women?" Neva asked.

"Like me."

"All are the same."

"No, I am a woman," said Mom. She sounded somewhat angry, somewhat embarrassed.

"You know, boys and girls," I said.

Neva blinked.

"I don't think it understands," I said. "Where Neva lives no one even has a name unless its master gives them one. This is probably not the time to teach about where boys and girls come from."

Mom nodded, though she was still feeling disturbed; I could tell. She would look out the sides of her eyes at times and blush as we waited for the others to arrive.

That night, I made sure we remained invisible, but the next morning, as we arose, I realized that the evening had been spent without disturbance. I got up from the floor, stretched, and made my way to the door. Peeking out momentarily, I was shocked at what I saw.

At least twenty men and women had gathered – not including the astronauts – and they were making their way up the stairs and into the interior of the plane.

I turned and woke my parents. Neva was already awake, and it blinked over at me.

"It's time," Neva said. "Your invisibility mechanism has dimmed. You are tired."

I wasn't sure about that, but I trusted Neva, I even looked to the plant as my source of strength and power. "What will we do?" I asked.

It was then that the door swung open and the woman in silver stepped in. "So, it is you," she said. "And you," she added staring at Neva with fire in her eyes. "I thought you'd be dead – by now."

"I was saved," Neva said softly.

"Only briefly," the woman offered. "Sit. I will know if you leave. You are only a shadow, but I can still see you."

"You cannot see us," I said. I thought of the compass, squeezed my eyes tight, and thought of the walls revealing themselves; of how I'd felt at the base of the mountain when Dad had told me what I needed to do to travel safely to this place.

The woman laughed. "And now we have almost everything we need to make the journey."

I turned to Neva. "What does she mean?" I asked.

Lost

Have you ever been lost? Not lost like you can't find your home, or you forgot where your classroom is, but really lost, lost inside your head.

Well, after feeling lost for a while myself in just this way, it came to me. I wasn't sure what or who had told me that the gift was mine forever, but it had just seemed to me that it was. My dad had asked me to use it to find our way back to the Green-Eyed Monster. It wasn't as if I'd forced anyone to give it to me; I'd just used it, and it had really helped us out.

We wouldn't have even found this place if it hadn't been for me. The walls had been removed and we'd seen the entire space plane because of my gift. I'd been happy to share it, to cover everyone with it like a warm blanket – to keep them safe.

Neva blinked over at me like a lost puppy. Mom still held my hand and Dad paced the room. We were fully visible now, and we would never be totally invisible again.

Neva had tried to explain it to me. The gift was to be used in purity; and mankind, well, they were about taking more than giving. Consider all of the people here who had finally taken away his invisibility for themselves until he couldn't find them anymore.

The plane and everything here would eventually vanish. It might be here for a time, sure, but no one would be able to feel it or to touch it.

I was angry. The last time I'd looked over at the space plane, it had resembled more of a fog. What were we going to do?

Dad stood. "Where is your friend?" he asked.

"He is here."

"Where?"

"In this room, but Neva will be gone soon."

Mom wiped at the tears in her eyes.

I stood, releasing Mom's hand. "So, I guess it's my fault!" I yelled. "Well, I've burned plenty of places down, why not this?!"

"What is burn?" Neva asked.

"Fire!"

"Fire? What is fire?"

"You're so stupid, do you know that? Fire! Hot! It burns down things! Makes them into ash! Girls and boys, men and women, they are different! You don't know anything!"

Neva shuddered, his mouth opening into an O where I could barely stuff swirling.

"Your mouth is stupid," I said.

87

Neva was silent. "Then, you do not want my love," it said.

"No, I don't!" I stomped to the corner of the room that was quickly fading and sat down.

Dad was still standing, still pacing. "Neva, my son tells me that you can heal. He tells me you can hear thoughts. What are you hearing now?"

"They are almost inside. They are waiting for someone."

"Who?"

Dad turned. He stared in Neva's direction in hope.

"One of the doctors; he hasn't arrived and they're trying to decide if they should leave without him."

I blinked.

Dad reached for the door. "Where are the aviation suits kept?" he asked.

"In the first room, but they might be hard to see by now."

"Tell me where they are."

Dad nodded. I wondered in the nod if Neva was speaking to Dad's mind and if he was acknowledging something. "All of you remain here. I have an idea. I may be able to escape this place and bring back the space plane. Do you trust me?"

I nodded, but I could see Mom was having a hard time of it. Her brown eyes had welled up like a mud puddle.

Dad opened the door with an unknown force I was to learn about later, looked around the corner, and made his way to the first room, still invisible to the others.

I didn't see Dad after that. Mom was past crying by then, and as the plane hummed, I hoped that all was not lost. Would we die on this planet, inside the caves, amazingly, almost like the others?

When the walls returned to their rightful place, I took Mom's hand. I'd long since forgiven Neva, blaming myself for the entire episode, but I would never be able to forgive myself. As we climbed up through the second entrance, and made our way out to the open air, I wiped at the tears that had accumulated on my cheeks.

Mom held me close, but I knew she missed Dad, and that it was my entire fault if we never saw him again – that is, if he'd made it to the plane in the first place. Had the space taken off without the doctor? Had my dad made it safely on board in his place before the thing had dwindled out of sight?

Perhaps we would never know.

The Shelter

"Do not worry. Your father is alright."

The words were said and I was relieved, though I couldn't see Neva anywhere.

And then, a coolness, like a plant that had just been watered, came upon my skin in an instant and was gone.

"Neva!"

Mom held me in her arms like a baby. I let her. Everything was ruined. Everything! And now Dad was gone, and Neva had evaporated because of me. It was there, and probably even speaking to me right now. But I would never hear from it again.

Mom sat and reached inside her bag. "We need to eat," she said.

"I'm sorry," I offered, looking up at the sky, taking in the heat of the afternoon. We sat under a tree, shadowing us from the brightest light, but I still felt the warmth melt into my bones. I took off my jacket. Mom did the same.

"You can't blame yourself." She began to peel her orange, not looking at me.

But I did blame myself; couldn't help but blame myself.

"So, if Dad's alright, where is he going?"

"On his way to the Rentaurus System more than likely."

"How far away is it?" I asked, watching as Mom peeled the remainder of her orange and took her first bite. "Good," she said.

"How far?" I was hungry but I didn't care. I had to know the facts, all of them.

"Trillions of miles from here. Your father will be old when he arrives."

"And we'll be dead," I said without thinking.

Mom turned her eyes to me. "Maybe that will be okay."

"What?" I snarled.

"He will be old, ready for death, and we will be dead already."

"How old?" I asked, trying to keep my voice down; for what, I had no idea.

"In his eighties, give or take."

Dad was already in his mid-thirties. So that meant he'd be traveling for fifty years. Why even go at all?

Mom took another bite of orange and smiled over at me. She seemed to guess my thoughts because I knew she couldn't read minds. "We were doing this for you," she said, wiping her fingers on a wet towel she'd also packed – a towel that never dried.

"Even though you knew you'd be old when we got there?"

Mom nodded.

Fifty years from now I would be sixty, and I didn't consider that a very great age to start a new life, but I didn't share these feelings with Mom. She was going through a hard enough time without Dad, and, besides, we would be dying here in less than a week.

The car was where Dad had last parked it, but it was no longer hidden. Mom stopped me with her hand as we rounded the corner, trying to hide me with her body (as if that would work) before we were spotted.

It was dusk, and the streets were quiet. But we weren't alone.

A hand touched my shoulder and yanked me forward even before I knew anyone was there. Mom was pulled away from me and she screamed – once – before being shoved in the back of the police car.

"What are you doing out here?" the police officer scolded.

"Nothing."

"We watched you descend all the way from the top of Ophir. Why were you up there? Haven't you heard?" He pushed me forward and led me to the front of his police car. It glinted a hazy blue in the quickly darkening sky.

He pushed me inside.

"Are you alright?" Mom asked from the back.

I nodded.

"Quiet! Why didn't you enter the shelter as instructed? You are right here. You couldn't have gotten lost."

"My son was afraid," Mom said, staring into her hands.

"Afraid of dying in there," I replied, looking over at the man.

"Well, you would have most assuredly died out in the elements. I suppose you figured that out."

I nodded.

"Where is your father?"

"I don't have a father," I lied, but the lie must not have been good enough or something because the police officer smiled. He had big teeth, and his left eye appeared to be a different color from his right. I'd heard all about these cops – transforming themselves into something un-Earthly – but until that night I hadn't really believed it. One eye was yellow and the other, blue, matching the vehicle.

The cop reached for the interior trap, a sort of small compartment where car screens were kept in case a person got pulled over, whether in the air or on the ground. He reached for it now and pushed a button.

"It says here that your father works at *Digitus Flight*. He is a *New American*."

"That's right," my mom said from the back seat. "But he is no longer with us."

"He's not dead, I've already checked the records."

"No, not... dead," my mom echoed. "He has left us."

"Where has he gone?"

"I... "

"Where has he gone?!"

"After the terrible news, he left us."

"You mean to tell me, that a man of high caliber, a *New American*, has left you and your son?"

"That's right."

The officer closed the screen. I'll have you know, ma'am, that your husband was working at *Digitus* just over a week ago and..."

"That's right. He was acting crazy. He told us to get into the car and he drove us here, got out of the vehicle, and told us to find shelter inside the school. He said he had something to do."

"I watched him walk away. It was terrible," I lied, trying to sniff just a bit for effect. It was terrible after all when I thought about it. Dad had really left us, but not on foot, and we might never see him again. Soon enough the tears were coming for real, and Mom was reaching for me.

"Now, see what you've done. My boy's frightened, that's all."

The police officer looked towards the mountains. "Did he make his way there?" he pointed.

My heart sank. How come I hadn't kept my big mouth shut? I thought of Neva's mouth now, all swirling inside with love, a love I hadn't wanted.

"Stay here."

The officer slid from the driver's seat and walked to the other officers nearby.

I turned to Mom. "It's alright," she said. "We'll figure something out."

"A lot of good that will do," I replied, looking out the passenger window. A family of four were making their way inside, their dog ushered to the side. All I could hear was barking.

Fear

You have probably felt fear before, the kind of fear that leaves you shaking in your boots. Say you've come face to face with a mountain lion, or your mom finds out you've been stealing or cheating on every school test. Maybe there's a bully in your school — one that hates everyone, and who isn't afraid to show it.

Don't hold your breath. What I'm about to tell you now will make your skin crawl and your eyes bug out. You may never want to eat again. Are you sitting down? I hope so.

Mom and I were taken to the school by another police officer. He had normal eyes and was full-blood human. I thought this might make it easier to escape; but looking into my Mom's eyes briefly, I knew I needed to follow her lead. I'd messed up too many times already.

It was almost dark. As we made our way through the doors of the school, down two long halls, and to the basement where I figured the shelter was, I took in a sickening smell. The room was big – about half the size of a football field – but it was full to overflowing. Everyone sat next to each other like sardines, children were crying, and it smelled like urine and other gross stuff. I looked for a toilet but didn't see one.

I looked above me and couldn't see the dome barrier I'd heard so much about. The roof looked more like plastic – thick plastic you might find on a cooling unit for your food. I tried to remember how the above ground domes had looked the few times I'd been in one during field trips and such, but there wasn't a comparison. With the above-ground domes, I'd always been able to see out. Now, all I could make out was the floor above.

I suddenly wondered if we were allowed to use the bathrooms upstairs, and how often. The walls were brick, the floor cement. Canned food lined one wall, along with more recent discoveries of food preservation, like *snap and click*, that I'd used myself. What looked like large jugs of water, were stacked against another wall. The room was lit by the newest in technology – a fan light (short for fantastic) that would never break, never need replacement, and always shine a bright white glow. People were sitting and sleeping on cots or on the floor in sleeping bags. I couldn't even count the people because there were so many. I imagined they must have flashlights somewhere or stuff that could fix a broken bone, but I didn't see anything like that.

The place was creepy like a ghost town with people in it.

I took Mom's arm as we made our way into the room and sat down. Five days from now Mercury would hit.

I don't know how many days passed, and no one told us. We got one bathroom break a day it seemed and were given a color. So far, I'd had three bathroom breaks. Mom and I were in the Aqua group. We ate and slept on cots near the canned food wall. There was nothing to do except sleep, talk, eat, and use the restroom when they'd let you. Mom and I always went when it was dark, but I don't know if it was morning or night.

I thought a lot about Dad during those days down in the shelter, and I thought about Neva and the Green-Eyed Monster in Ophir Canyon. I thought about Slew – the one my parents had met that hadn't been named yet – and I thought about Bronty. I worried about my best friend. But there was nothing I could do.

You have to know I was very depressed, even more depressed than when my dog had died and when Bronty had first left for Mars. I don't know what it was, but it was probably because of the smells, the crying, and the whining of people around me that did it. Plus, I had no freedom to do anything.

I wondered then, as I have wondered since, what was so all-fire important about taking safety in a bomb shelter if we were going to die anyway. I'd learned in school that the shelters had been built in the 1960s for the fallout – the radioactive dust – and not for the blast of the bomb itself. I couldn't help wondering how any of us could live through a planet crashing into Earth, maybe even two, if the news was right, though we had a dome barrier.

I clung to Mom and tried to cheer her up with jokes about bananas that slid in the dark and mushrooms that bloomed like flowers. Mom would laugh, but I knew the laugh was fake and for me. We talked about Dad and we spoke about our lives together before coming here. Even going into the cave and getting caught was better than this.

I don't know when it first occurred to me that something was changing. When I'd had my fourth bathroom break, I began to see the room differently.

It was weird, you know?

Do you remember the Green-Eyed Monster cave and the one that looked plain, when in fact it was housing an invisible space plane? That's how I began to think about the shelter. I thought about it not having any ceiling or walls. I started thinking this was because I realized, for the first time, that the space plane had left the cavern, and lifted into the air, without any walls, without a ceiling.

And then I thought of something else. What if, through stealing Neva's invisibility, the astronauts had actually found a way to escape through rock?

If the space plane was there, but not there, it would be an easy way to leave the cavern. And you know, the astronauts wouldn't have built it in that cavern in the first place if they hadn't known that there was a way of escape.

I turned to Mom. She was sleeping, but my head was swirling. I could even see the Green-Eyed Monster's mouth, Neva's mouth, swirling in my head – swirling with love.

Maybe what I was seeing in the underground shelter really wasn't what was here. And if not, why... I could leave whenever I wanted. And I could take Mom!

So, you think I'm crazy?

I did too. At least, at first.

I thought about it some more as the people snored around me and the babies cried; I thought about a way out.

"Neva, Neva, can you hear me?" I spoke into the room.

"Silence!" Someone nearby twisted in their bed and returned to sleep.

"Neva!" I said in my mind. "Neva!"

"Aaden. Is that you?"

"Where are you?"

"On your shoulder…"

"On my…" Tears filled my eyes upon this surprising revelation, but then again, maybe I shouldn't have been surprised. Neva hadn't left me since it had found me.

"We need to get out of here."

"I know."

"Why haven't you said anything?" I yelled inside my mind.

"I have."

"When?"

"Every moment. Every day!"

"But when? I haven't…"

In the next breath, small, so as not to die from the stench, I thought about what Neva had said. Instead of speaking I listened. So, that was it.

"I'm sorry," I said.

Neva was silent.

"And I'm sorry about how I treated you."

Someone snorted from behind me, but I tried to remain focused.

"I know. Are you ready?" it said.

I couldn't help it. I started to cry. I used to think that only lame, wimpy kids cried, but I had seen my dad cry. I knew that if he could cry so could I.

When Mom awoke, I spoke softly to her as the meal was passed out. It was canned chili today and I really didn't want to have anything to do with chili and its aftereffects if you know what I mean. According to my records – more in memory than anything else – today was day five, the day of death.

Mom nodded as I spoke to her about Neva's plan. It would be simple.

I could feel the warmth filling my body as Neva shared with me his gift of invisibility. Since he knew that I was sorry, Neva was happy to share the gift again. I had only heard him because I had begun to forgive myself, and I was able to receive the light of invisibility because I was willing to listen. The same healing was done for Mom.

And then we stood, making our way to the door. It took only a thought about being invisible, and I knew others could not see us. It was like they looked right through us. One child, intent on getting to its mother, actually knocked into me, and looking up and seeing no one, continued forward. But I could smell its wet diaper, and I was more than happy to get out of there. The guards only blinked at the emptiness they believed was there, and Mom and I walked past them, up the stairs, down the two halls, and out the front door where four other guards were standing. They didn't see us either.

We walked in the direction of where our car had once been parked and it was no longer there. Touching Neva's leg, I asked, "Now, what's the plan? Where are we going?"

Neva was silent for a moment and then its tinny voice filled my ears. "Look uppppp," it said. At that moment, I realized how dark it was, and how silent. There didn't appear to be a living plant anywhere other than Neva. I was reminded of those old cowboy movies, right before the two men make their paces forward. We were here, now, when the Earth was quiet, waiting for its imminent future. In only moments, Mercury would hit.

"Take your Mom's hand," Neva said.

We were standing in the middle of the school parking lot, and there was no time to find safety now – no time to find a shuttle or a space plane – though the thoughts of sneaking aboard one had been on my mind for many hours. It was too late.

Everything, and I mean everything happened in slow motion after that. The skies, now darkening, revealed something in the sky – a large eye. No, it was more like a huge, round ball – gray.

After the darkness, I saw it – Mercury – as it expanded to my view. I could even make out the blue pockmarks, like the worse ache problem imaginable in the wrong color, growing larger and larger in front of me. I don't know what I expected to see and feel during my last moments on Earth, but this wasn't it.

The Earth rumbled hard and fast then. If you've ever been on a roller coaster, one of those old ones that clank around the tight turns or heard the rumbling sound of an old washing machine when the loaded clothes are unbalanced, you might know what I'm talking about. That was what I was hearing now, only intensified.

"Be still," Neva said. I could feel its cold hand on my cheek. "When the planet hits, remember my love for you."

"Will we die?" I whispered, hardly trusting my voice, but knowing that I had to say something.

"Be still."

I looked into my mom's eyes. She was crying, little rivulets of tears falling from her cheeks. "I love you, Aaden," she said.

I closed my eyes, letting my own tears drip down my cheeks. I don't know how long I stood there with my mom and Neva, but it seemed like an eternity. I felt the love of Neva like never before, and a sort of calmness.

When the mass hit, I opened my eyes, watching it – somehow – as if the experience was merely on a movie wall screen. My body didn't move, neither did my mom's, but the Earth all around us was in commotion. I heard screaming first, from the hole of the shelter, and then suddenly rocks, buildings, trees, even pets, were flying through the air, swept into the sky like the greatest tornado ever.

The sky spun and appeared to eat everything that wasn't firmly attached, and that meant everything. The top of the school, now gone, revealed men, women, and children from the basement, clutching one another, walls, and trees as they flew out.

I couldn't look.

Suddenly, water was at my feet, but not like the water from the cavern. This water grew thicker by the minute. Still, I didn't move. It was like the greatest last days movie on surround view and I was a part of it. It appeared that none of the elements could touch me. Water surrounded my legs, but I did not feel wet. Air zipped around me like a tornado, but I didn't feel a thing.

I remembered the words of Neva, felt its presence on my shoulder, and clutched my mom's hand with all I had until the terror stopped.

Sore Eyes

My mom not only kept things in her house that belonged in a junkyard but said things that had been un-said for years. *A sight for sore eyes* was one of them. Her mother used to say it, and before that, *her* mother. I'd heard all of the stories – sore eyes when my relatives hadn't seen me for a long time, sore eyes when I'd finally managed to clean myself up – you know, but that afternoon, after Mercury hit, sending people and things everywhere, there were no words to describe what I was feeling.

For it wasn't long after Mercury's demise, that another shock wave hit the Earth. This time an explosion of rock hit everything still moving. I remembered Mars, and what Dad had said about the planet's lopsided orbit and how the planet would break apart in the sky and shower the Earth like heavy rain.

I was glad I couldn't feel it. Somehow, with some terrific power that I could have only hoped to possess, Neva's power had saved us. It was like an invisible barrier was wrapped around me, like plastic wrap, only thicker, and although I couldn't see it, I could feel the difference.

I looked at the school that had once been a part of my life. All was silent, and I knew that Mom, Neva and I were the only ones who had survived – at least here where I could see. I tried not to think of all of the others throughout the world in similar shelters with dome barriers, but I just couldn't keep the thoughts from me, nor the vision of people and things – no longer living – floating beside me.

For a moment, everything had stopped. I looked around me. Nothing was as it should have been. Nothing. The entire view before me looked like something from an alien takeover. Everything was leveled. Cars. Trees. Houses.

Huge chunks of rock from the planet were scattered around me. Roads were split and thrown to the side like someone had taken a big knife and sliced them down the middle. Water was everywhere, and it was almost as high as my waist.

"It's time to return to the Green-Eyed Monster."

"The mountain?"

Neva nodded.

I tightened my bag around my shoulders and smiled over at Mom.

She had been silent through the entire episode and she was silent now as we slushed our way through the water I could not feel and returned to the mountain that I'd climbed up and back twice already.

As we reached the summit, I realized that it had been easier this last time but for an entirely different reason. This time, Neva had traveled with us, but I also knew, looking down, that the Earth would never be the same again.

My clothes had not gotten wet through the journey, but they were still dirty, and for the first time I wondered when I'd be able to wear a clean pair of pants again.

We were visible; there was no reason to hide now, and as we looked down from the mountain, I wondered how long we could live like this.

"The Earth has stopped its rotation, and we are in light shade," Neva said, looking up. "See the sky?"

The sky was strange, almost like a flat canvas with smoke and dust that covered the blue I was used to seeing. I thought of the word light shade, and wondered what Neva meant.

"The air pattern has changed. Feel it?"

I shrugged.

"I feel it," Mom said.

I looked at her, really looked at her this time. Her hair was a mess; her clothes full of dirt including her fingernails.

"Mom, you're filthy," I said.

"You're a sight for sore eyes yourself," she said, making me laugh, if only briefly because I'd just been thinking about it.

I turned to Neva. It was standing across from me. "Thank you," I said.

"Yes," Mom echoed, reaching out her hand.

The plant didn't take it. Instead, it opened its mouth, green swirls within it.

"That means that Neva loves you," I said.

Mom touched her cheek, wiping away a tear. "I feel it," she said.

I reached inside my bag and took out the last orange. We all sat. I still had a little water, but not enough to quench my thirst. My mom opened her bag and took out a sandwich. "Want this?" she asked, "I'm not hungry."

I waved her away.

"Are you sure?"

I was sure I was hungry, but not hungry enough to eat the last thing in Mom's bag. She didn't even have water.

"Hey, why don't we share my water," I said, setting it beside her.

"Thanks."

As we ate, Neva gathered pieces of tree trunk – the planets had taken down many – and I was grateful beyond belief that we'd somehow escaped death. Pulling the bark from a tree, I watched as it sucked out the sap. In time, Neva's color returned.

After eating, we found our way to the cavern, but could not get inside. There was no longer an opening.

"Maybe that won't matter," said Neva, as I thought on the last time I had seen my dad. It seemed like so long now, though it had only been a week.

"What did you need?" Mom asked.

"A map; something to tell us in what direction the other space planes are hidden."

"A lot of good that will do – now," I said. I guess the comment was a bit sarcastic. Mom looked at me from the corner of her eye and Neva was silent.

"Sorry," I said. "What makes you think there are still some planes here?"

"It's just a feeling."

I rolled my eyes before I caught myself.

"Your mom is more than likely right," Neva said. "Slew and I are not the only two Rentauriun plants..."

"About that," I began before Neva had time to continue, "that's where the space planes were heading, right?"

Neva nodded and sucked out a bit more sap from the pine at its lap.

"How did they discover the planet? What's its name anyway?"

"Taurus."

"You mean like the star constellation?"

Neva smiled awkwardly. "Of course, but the planet itself isn't in your solar system."

"So, why is it named Taurus?"

"Many moons ago, before you or even your mom was born, we traveled here, liked what we saw in the northern sky, and decided to name our planet after the great bull. Taurus' red eye was the best part – it reminded us of the red soil on our own home world..."

"Which was named what before you changed it to Taurus?"

Neva looked confused. His skin paled slightly and his one green eye blinked.

"Name?"

"Yeah. Before it was the planet Taurus."

"It didn't have a name."

"That's weird," I said.

Mom nudged me. "I think it makes perfect sense," she said. "So, a human must have named it."

"That's right," Neva answered, directing its eye in my mom's direction. "Unfortunately, the human that named it is dead, and all we have now are humans that steal our identity."

"You mean your gifts?" I asked.

Neva sucked in another bit of sap. "Yesssss," it said. "Once the humans in silver figured out that they could steal my invisibility, they went about trying to find other things to steal, but by then we were too smart."

"So, they didn't get your healing and mind reading gifts," I said.

"No. As far as any of them knew, invisibility was our only gift."

"So, are there humans on your planet?"

Neva paled even more. "Yes… but everything was taken from us and we had to find shelter elsewhere."

I thought of my dad and the others traveling to Taurus within the Rentaurus System and wondered what they would think once they landed only to discover they weren't the first humans to arrive.

"They will be surprised," Neva said, reading my thoughts. "Very surprised."

"Are the other humans, like us?" Mom asked.

"Sadly, yes, though they are much more advanced than the humans here. I tried to tell the men in silver, but they wouldn't listen. As the years passed, and the space planes were built, they were happy to do things on their own without me – well, until others started finding the cavern where I found you. When your civilization was finally advanced enough to travel to the Rentaurus System, and ultimately, Taurus, and when the others decided they could learn nothing more from us, we were pretty much discarded."

"And Slew?" I asked.

"It is still alive. And it's not on the space plane."

I blinked.

"It is not on the space plane and neither is your father."

I don't know why I was so angry, but I was. If Neva had known my dad was alive, why hadn't it said something sooner?

Neva shrugged. "So sorry. We had to get up the mountain. We had to be free of the water."

"But you could have told us!"

Mom wiped tears from her eyes. They'd welled up without me even noticing. "So, I was right," she said.

My eyes were like hot stones. "What, you knew too?"

"I wondered." Mom smiled, wiping a tear away. "Aaden, Neva is right. We couldn't have stayed there. We had to get above the water."

"So, where is he?" I asked.

"I was hoping the cavern opening hadn't fallen in. I didn't want to say anything until I…"

"What?" My hands shook. I reached for Mom's hand. "Then he's dead then," I said.

It was the first time I'd said the words and they hurt more than falling while climbing up the mountain, more than Bronty leaving me for good.

"Slew is here," Neva said, "and I feel the presence of your father with it."

"Here?" Mom asked.

"They have survived within the cavern."

I looked over at the closed-up hole and wondered how. And then I remembered how we'd been saved. "Slew has the same powers as you," I said. "Of course."

Neva nodded. "They are being protected. But unlike us, they were not in an open area when the planet hit. It takes much power to receive safety within the walls of the Green-Eyed Monster."

"But a space plane went through it."

"The men in silver, using Slew's powers, and perhaps the powers of another, barely escaped the limestone, but before that moment, Slew tells me that he had just enough invisibility left to bring your father back."

"What?"

"I wanted to go myself, return to my homeland, just like you want to return home to the place of you're a… birth, but I was mistaken. Those who reach Taurus will not be happy with their decision. Better to live on a broken planet than not to have a name."

I couldn't believe a name meant so much, but I didn't say anything. I stood, walked over to the cavern that had only had a small entrance, and now none. "Can't we go through the walls?" I asked.

"Soon. I am regaining my strength."

Mom's head lifted then. She smiled through her tears. "How long?" she asked.

KATHRYN ELIZABETH JONES

The Iron Pillar

A day later, and Neva's powers of invisibility were still weak. The plant ate tree sap like it was going out of business, and we tried to find wild things to eat like berries, pine nuts, pine needles and wild violets. Yes, we'd started to eat purple flowers.

Now, before you start getting grossed out, you need to know that water was gone by the second day on the mountain. We had begun to lick off the leaves of plants where dew accumulated in the morning, but that was about the extent of our liquid intake.

By the second afternoon, all I wanted to do was sit under a pine tree and do nothing. I had hateful thoughts for Neva again. I felt like, if nothing else, the plant would be able to heal us hourly and we wouldn't have to go through all of this pain.

I thought I'd been hungry before, but not like this. It wasn't like I'd missed a meal because I was sent to bed because of my bad behavior. It wasn't even like fasting and cleansing your body for a meal or two; you know not eating and hoping to get closer to God because you're going without food. No, this was different. As I watched my mom sleep under the old pine tree, I followed suit, laying my head on her belly and stretching my legs out in front of me.

I must have slept because when I opened my eyes, my mom was no longer underneath me, but the skies were still light – as if night hadn't arrived all. It was a long howl that had probably woken me up, and I knew instantly that another creature had joined us.

"It's a bear," Mom whispered, taking my hand in hers. Neva must have been sitting on my shoulder or it was out foraging for more pine tree sap because I didn't see it. The air was still hot, still baking down my back.

Mom wrapped her arm around me. "We need to be still," she said, "so still, the bear will think we're dead."

I breathed in slowly, feeling dead already and wondering how the bear could have been alive. With all of the dead surrounding us, how had it remained un-hurt?

I could hear the bear even before I saw it. It moaned deep in its throat and clacked its teeth. I could hear it sniffing for us. When its body swooshed near, pieces of tree branch crackling under its paws, Mom held me tightly, not speaking.

Even though we held still I wondered if the bear could see us.

"Just sit still," Mom said.

The bear sniffed again, a deep-throated moan escaping its lips.

I shivered. A tear slid down my cheek and dropped to my neck. I wanted to yell out, scream for Neva, do something – run away – but Mom held me fast. I felt like a two-year-old, wrapped in its mother's arms, but I didn't care.

I'm not sure how long we sat in this position, listening to the bear who obviously knew we were there, its red eyes burning into my own; not moving until we no longer heard it. But it was long enough for me.

I could feel Mom relax her arms around me when the bear had moved far enough away from us. She brushed my hair with her hand. "Are you all right?" she asked.

When I was silent, she asked again: "Aaden, are you, all right?"

"Yes," I said.

"Good."

"I'm glad you're alrighttttt." Hearing Neva's voice did not soothe me. "Where were you?" I asked, still not standing, not daring to.

"On your shoulder, as always."

"Then why…"

I wiped at the tears that were still flowing down my neck, wiped them with the back of my hand and waited for Neva to say something. It didn't.

"You can't blame Neva," Mom said. "I don't know how the bear managed to escape death, but Neva couldn't have done anything to save us anyway."

"And why not? It… it has powers!" I sniffed.

"I have just enough to re-open the entrance and save your father," Neva said. "And yours, well, you used the little you had left to get us here."

So, I had done it again – let my anger out. I wanted to take the words back but I couldn't. Neva probably hated me, and for the first time, I really cared. I was a horrible friend.

"Sorry," I said, but Neva didn't answer. Instead, Neva led us to the cave's entrance. I reached for Mom's hand.

"You must trust me," It said.

I wondered for the second time how the bear had survived the collision of Mercury and the debris of Mars, but there wasn't time to ask. Instead, we listened as Neva led us into the Green-Eyed Monster.

In seconds, we were beyond the outer wall, and making our way through the limestone. A few footsteps later, I could see the green wall that looked like crystal. It was smaller than I remembered it, the limestone walls around it holding it close. We were still within the limestone – there was no mistaking it. But there was also no breathing space. If not for Neva, Mom and I would never have been able to survive in there.

"Take a piece," Neva directed.

"But you said…" In a split second, I was remembering my first visit when I hadn't been allowed to touch the green treasure, and now… I could?

"Take a piece. Hurry."

Reaching forward, I touched the green stone, prying a loose piece from the large embroidery of green. I brought it to my eyes, looking at the light within it.

"There is a crack in everything," Neva smiled crookedly. "And we are in light shade."

"I can see that," I said, understanding coming to my mind and heart. We lived on the light side of the Earth now; there were others in the shade.

"Even in terror, great things can come to pass."

"You sound just like my Bible," I said, seeking the light with even more fervency. Suddenly, it was as if the green light entered my soul. Chills raced up my arms and to my head and down my legs. It was like I was cold and warm at the same time.

"What does it do?"

I looked over at mom briefly. She was staring at the stone, her mouth open.

"It will save all of us."

Once we were out of the cavern, I turned to Neva for further answers. It instructed me to put the green stone into my bag. This time, unlike other times when I thought I knew better, I listened to Neva. I opened the closest pocket, placed the stone inside, and pushed the flap shut.

"Thank you," Neva whispered, taking my hands. Its small hands were clammy, would always be clammy. It was like Neva was a plant with legs. As long as it was watered – perhaps the tree sap did that – and as long as no one stole anything from it, like the plant's powers of invisibility, Neva would be free to help them always.

"So, where is my dad?" I asked.

Mom was sitting beside me, and Neva was next to her.

"We need to travel back inside, but more resting is needed."

"Why? Can't the green stone help?"

"You are not yet ready."

I almost rolled my eyes, but then I caught myself. "What do I need to do?" I asked. Frankly, it was getting hotter than blazes outside, even with the shaded barrier that Neva provided, and I needed a drink of water.

Sensing my thoughts, Neva took me by the hand. "There is water nearby, but you must trust me."

I nodded and looked back at Mom. She looked about as weak as that time she'd had the flu and couldn't keep anything down – weaker if that's possible.

"Is there any way you two can bring the water back to me? Just fill my jug." She reached in her bag and pulled out her water jug. I took it. "Are you sure?" I asked.

Mom smiled slightly, lying down. We were once again under the tree, and if the truth be told, I wanted a nap too. My tongue felt like a dried branch. Maybe Neva would share some tree sap with me.

Neva must have heard my thoughts because it laughed. "Oh, no you don't. I can't make it to the water without you. You must come."

"How far?" I asked.

"See that rise over there?"

I peered in the direction of Neva's three fingers. Sure enough, there was a rise, like a new mountain had risen up even higher than where we were sitting. "How did that happen?" I asked.

"The Earth, it will never be the same again," said Neva, jumping onto my shoulder. "And it's up to us to make a difference."

"Is everyone dead?" I asked, taking my mom's hand briefly and kissing it. But she was already asleep.

"No. But most are gone. Your father and Slew have only hours yet."

"Can you see what they are doing?"

Neva was silent for a moment. "No," it said, "but I know where they are. We must all receive the strength to get them. We all must go."

122

I couldn't figure it out. I thought about all of Neva's powers. I thought about it going alone into the cavern and retrieving my dad and Slew, but I kept my thoughts to myself as far as I was able, and Neva was silent as we walked the new terrain of the mountain.

By the time it was supposed to be dark, I decided not to look at the torn trees, huddled in masses as if, even they, lived in fear. I didn't have to look at the emptiness. The strewn grasses, the silence of the canyon.

At the water's edge, I placed my jug into the wet stream and gathered what I could, filling Mom's jug as well. "I wish we had more jugs," I said.

"I wish I could share my sap with you," offered Neva.

"How will we survive?" I asked. My stomach growled suddenly as if in response. Neva jumped from my shoulder and stood before me. "Sit," it said, "and take out your flashlight."

I sat, reached in the bag, and quickly found the metal flashlight. It was one of the world's newest advancements – a flashlight of light metal alloy – and although I didn't understand all of the mechanics, I knew the thing would never rust, would never wear, would always look as good as the day my dad had brought it home to me. Most of all, it would never feel heavy no matter how long I carried it.

"When the men came, and the women…" Neva smiled slightly and continued, "I thought they were fools to want to build inside a cavern where anything metal inside it would rust. But then I realized they'd finally figured out the secret of Delhi."

"The secret of Delhi?"

Neva brushed its hand against its face, its large eye staring. "You do not know your history," it said. "Long ago, in the times of the Gupta kings, a metal was discovered that would never rust. Those of Delhi used it to their glory, the Iron Pillar of Delhi being one of their greatest masterpieces."

"What did they use it for?" I asked.

"Not everyone knows or can comprehend the use of the iron pillar, and many have tried to read the inscriptions thereon. Consider: It rises from the Earth 23 feet."

"Wow. Something like that would be really heavy."

"Usually, Aaden. It was placed within the city of modern Delhi by the Tomar King."

"The who?"

"What's important here," Neva said softly as if someone might hear us, "is that the pillar has not rusted in two thousand years and is so light and transportable that it could be carried to Delhi."

"But that's" – I was about to say 'impossible' when I stopped myself.

"What do you think your flashlight is made of?"

I looked closer at the flashlight, felt the weight of it in my hand. I could never figure that part out,

124

though I'd never said the same to anyone but myself. "It's light," I said.

"Not even half an ounce," Neva muttered. It stood and jumped back onto my shoulder. "We'd better get back," the plant said.

No Darkness

Mom was still resting when we returned. She was lying on her side, one of her arms under her head like a pillow. I reached into my bag and brought out one of the two jugs of water. That's when it came to me. As I placed the jug's lip under Mom's mouth and she drank, I almost spilled the liquid as I thought about Neva's healing powers, the powers it hadn't used.

"I hear your thoughts," Neva said suddenly. Mom sat up and took me in her arms. "Remember, everything is needed to save your father – and Slew."

I was amazed at myself. I would forget everything, perhaps even burn everything down, if it wasn't for people or non-people helping me to think straight.

"Sorry," I said again.

"We are almost ready," said Neva. "By morning."

I didn't think I could wait until morning, although it still felt like day. Suffice it to say, I had discovered the awful truth. We were on the lit side of the earth, and the others, they were on the dark side. When the Earth had stopped rotating, everyone was left to bake or die a frozen death. Life now was truly light or shade.

It was morning, but the sun beat on me like a huge iron skillet from the olden days. I thought about what Neva had told me as I gathered up my bag and placed it around my shoulders. Mom stood. She embraced me once. Neva hopped on my shoulder. "Forward!" it said.

At the mouth, or what once had been the mouth of the cave, I stopped. "Can I go in?" I asked.

"It's time," Neva said.

I don't know if I can begin to describe how utterly bizarre it was to walk within the walls of the green cavern – the Green-Eyed Monster – but in moments, like the day before, we were inside, though there was no space to be standing where we were, no oxygen to breathe in, smack dab within the limestone rocks.

"Now, through the tunnel," Neva said.

"This time, we didn't need to slither on our stomachs like snakes to get to the other side of the cave where the space plane had remained hidden in plain sight. We walked. I couldn't feel anything. Not the rock. Not the coolness of being underground. In moments, we were at the other end of the tunnel. All that was before me was rock. Just rock.

"I don't see anyone," I said. "Are you sure?"

"Shhhhh…" The sound of Neva's voice made me stop and take notice. "Grab the green stone."

I opened the pocket and reached for the stone. Laying it within my hand, I looked down at it.

"See the slight crack?" Neva asked.

I looked closer but couldn't see anything.

"Near the edge; *there*."

The rock glowed like a hundred flashlights as I search for the crack. I spun the thing over and over in my hands. My mom must have been watching because I could feel her hot breath on my neck. "This?" I said, pointing to a slight crack about as thin as a piece of straw.

"Yes! That's all it takes, a crack for the light to get in. Hold it up to the wall!"

I held the glowing gem above my head, though I wasn't sure what wall Neva spoke of. We were surrounded by walls!

"No, *there*!" Neva pointed its fingers in the direction of the most important wall that didn't appear different than any other wall. I was feeling pretty powerful like I was Superman or something; but I did as Neva instructed. Suddenly, a ray of light sprang forth from the dark surface and entered my eyes. "Ouch!" I said.

"Don't close your eyes! Wait!"

But I had already closed my eyes. The stone dropped to the cavern floor. In an instant, Neva must have been off my shoulder. It handed the stone back to me. I couldn't see anything, but I could feel the stone in the palm of my hand.

"Try again!" Neva muttered. "Open your eyes!"

I don't know if I can explain to you what happened next. I saw nothing but darkness. The light was gone. I couldn't see the stone and I could no longer see the light that had blinded me. I didn't know what to say or do, so I just stood there with the rock that I couldn't see, and the light that had suddenly dimmed – just stood there until someone brushed the tears from my eyes.

Mom.

I was in the dark.

Outside the cavern, I cried. Mom held me. I could not see anything. Not my mom. Not Neva. Not my hands in front of my face. I could feel the heat on my cheeks, the thirst in my throat, and the way the others sat silently because I had failed.

My mom spoke first. "It's not your fault," she began. "We should have explained everything."

"Everything? What?" I asked. And then something else came into my mind. My Mom had said 'we.'

"Mom?"

She held me close.

"You said 'we.'"

"That's right."

"What do you know about the cavern that you're not telling me?"

Mom was silent. "You must be healed," she said. "Let – "

"Mom, Neva will need its strength to find Dad."

Neva was silent.

"Mom?"

"Yes, Aaden?"

"Won't Neva need its strength?"

My mom's voice was as silent as the stream I'd dipped our water jugs in just yesterday. Perhaps it wasn't a stream at all that we'd gotten the water from, I thought suddenly. More like a puddle, a large puddle. "Neva," I said, "you do not need to heal me. At least not now. My dad… your friend, Slew…"

A cold hand pressed against my arm.

"I'm serious. Can you go back inside with Mom and find Dad?"

Neva shifted nervously, grains of earth moving to the side of me. "No," it said. "We need you."

"Why?"

Mom held me close. "You are the only one with the gift."

Now I was truly going crazy. What gift? Had the sun gotten to both of them? I was feeling it now through my shirt, my pants, yes, even my shorts. I knew we were under the shade of the tree, the shade of Neva's power, but not the shade of the planet. With Earth's halted rotation we were in the thick of it. The other side, they were probably wrapping a million blankets around them even now – unless they were dead.

"You are *Someone Like Fire*," Mom said.

I took the words in and tossed them inside my brain. "Sure," I said, a few moments later. "My name means 'someone like fire.'"

"You are '*Someone Like Fire*.' I am '*Tender*'. My name is Fonda."

I knew my mom's name was Fonda, though perhaps you didn't. But you need to know that before that moment, I had only thought of mom as Mom. "And Dad? Jachin?" I asked.

"*He that strengthens*."

"You act as if you knew about Neva even before I did," I managed, though my tongue was dry and my thoughts whirled inside my brain like crazy comics.

"I did," Mom said.

So, what would you do if you discovered your mom and dad had been lying to you? I'd heard stories about kids finding out they were adopted after they'd been living with their parents for a century; I'd even heard stories about the Easter Bunny, but this? Mom and Dad knew Neva? How could that be, unless...

I blinked my eyes, but I still couldn't see anything but darkness.

"Neva... Slew before that, met up with your father at the cave five years ago. Unlike the others, your dad had no desire to steal the gifts that Neva held.

"So, Dad told you about Neva?"

Mom was silent.

"What else do you know that you haven't told me?"

"I suppose it's time we talked about your gift," Mom said, choosing not to answer my question about Neva.

"That would be nice." My voice sounded funny but I didn't care. I felt so cheated I could hardly stand it.

"Your eyes are stronger than you think. Like fire," Mom said.

"So, why am I blind?" I offered.

"We should have prepared you," Neva offered, jumping down from my shoulder and more than likely staring up at me although I couldn't see it. "Now, we will."

"What do I have to do?" I asked, standing up. All I could see was black.

"I will heal your eyes," Neva said from below. "And you can save us."

I'm not sure I still believe what happened next. But my dad's life and the life of Slew were at stake. I didn't want Mom to die, and I wanted to live out my life until I got old.

"It takes faith," Neva said.

"I know all about faith," I countered, thinking about all of the lessons I'd sat through in church. I knew all about faith preceding the miracle. I knew about faith being something you couldn't see but that it could be felt with your heart. I knew that even if faith was as small as a mustard seed, great things could happen. I knew all about it.

"Faith takes great humility," Neva said.

"I know I can do it."

"No – humble," Mom said, jerking me from my thoughts.

I sat. "So, I'm not so humble," I said.

"Remember how you got angry at me for a time?" Neva asked.

I nodded. I felt sick inside.

"Remember how the men and... women took my power and never gave it back?"

"That's why we are in this mess," I said.

"Right." Neva's breath was close to my cheek. For the first time, I could truly smell it, like a plant getting the moisture it needed and the sunlight it craved. Except now, now it was too hot – too hot!

"Where's the water?" I asked.

Someone handed me a jug and I drank. In seconds, it was gone.

"We need to do this fast," said Neva. "You must listen." I recalled all of the times my parents had demanded I listen, and for the first time, it hit me how right they had been.

"Okay, what do I do?"

Light

The process, if you can call it that, was simple – perhaps too simple – but I tried not to doubt and be believing. As Neva healed my eyes, I saw anew the world in which I'd taken for granted. Yes, it was a mess, but there was still the sky, some green, even some water and food if one went out of one's way to find it.

"Your thoughts must be clear, with no other objective than to reach for others. The power cannot be for yourself. The minute you begin to think about the power being for you, or you begin to get angry, it will evaporate."

"That's why you let those men and women have your power," I said. "They took it, and you let them because it was not yours to use on yourself."

"Yes."

A large tear dripped from my right eye. I stood again, surveying the new mountain where we'd obtained water. I looked at my mom and my new friend, Neva. I thought about what Neva had said and about what my mom had kept secret.

"The fire from my eyes can burn stone then?"

"No. Something even better," said my mom. "When you were born, and when the fires began, your father and I couldn't believe it at first. Do you remember the time you were sitting all alone in your room and a fire sprang up on your bed?"

"What?" I asked, flabbergasted.

"You were five."

"What happened?" I asked, not remembering anything.

"When I smelled the smoke and raced into your room you were standing in the corner. Your bed looked just like a bonfire. Fortunately, your father was able to put it out before it spread up the curtains."

"Fortunately," I mumbled.

"And then there was the time we were camping and you used your eyes to start the kindling. You were eight then."

"I think I remember that," I said, searching my mind for the picture, the moment. "But I thought Dad started the fire. He showed me the 'wonder' match."

Mom smiled. "That was only to protect you."

I tried to remember the fire in the kitchen, how it had started. I tried to remember the fire in the tree house. "You mean..."

"Exactly," Neva muttered. "But we must go – now."

Neva hopped on my shoulder and together we walked to the cave's opening.

"With control, your gift will burn this cavern in a different way. The surface will simply disappear."

"How?"

"You know that warmth you get inside when you're doing something great?"

I thought of heartburn first, but that didn't make sense. "You mean when I think of reaching out?"

"Yes. This is where you go."

"Why didn't you tell me this before?" I asked.

Mom was silent. "It was the only way," she finally said. "You needed to know that the other way wouldn't work."

"You mean, thinking I was Superman?"

"Is that what happened?" Neva asked, though I knew it knew the truth.

I nodded, lifting the green stone above my head, thinking of all those I loved. All it took was a crack for the light to get in. I thought again and again of Dad, and how much he meant to me. I thought of Mom and Slew and Neva – even Bronty. And when the wall to the outside of the cavern lit and it began to burn my eyes, I kept looking, even when darkness came and I wanted to shut my eyes. I didn't close them. I waited.

It seemed like forever, but as I stood at the outside of the Green-Eyed Monster, I felt such love inside that I don't think I can explain to you. It was as if all the worry, all the pain, all the hate, all the plain and simple stupid stuff that I'd done in my entire life drifted away, and in its place, was family.

"Son!" Dad stumbled toward me. Slew was sitting nearby, and I could see its crooked smile upon me. I knew about this crooked smile, and I smiled back.

Aliens

So, it seems I was mistaken.

I was not born on planet Earth, but Taurus, within the Rentaurus System. But how? It took travelers two and a half months to get to Mars from here, and Taurus was even further away than that.

"You told me it would take fifty years to travel from Earth to Taurus," I said, not believing that I was from another galaxy, another planet – that I was in fact – an alien. "How old were you when you left the planet? You're not even fifty years old now."

Dad blinked at me and looked over at Mom.

"What I told you was the truth," Dad said. "Getting here was easy. Quick. Leaving, I'm afraid, is going to be much harder."

"Why?"

"We made a mistake."

"What kind of mistake?"

"One that we couldn't easily correct," Mom said, placing her arm around me.

I shrugged it off.

"A few of us arrived thinking we could save Earth. We thought…" Mom looked over at Dad, and a small tear creased her eye. "We thought we could save the planet. We thought…"

"After we arrived and construction began – we arrived when you were just little, son – we soon discovered the problem. The metals used on Taurus are heavier here. We had to reconstruct the space planes, and that meant finding a metal on Earth that would be light enough to carry the humans into space. For years, we tried and failed to construct the space planes with the metals here, finally finding one we thought would work. Still, though the metal was light, the space plane did not have the thrust to get us out of the Earth's atmosphere. We were stuck."

"But with all your knowledge…"

"Never underestimate doing your homework," Mom said. "Never assume anything."

"So, there is no way off?"

I thought of attempting to leave the only home I knew, getting taken by the men and women, the *New Americans*, the times of hunger and thirst. So, I'd done this all for nothing?

"Maybe not," Dad said, following me out. We sat on the grass – what was left of it – and Dad stared up at the sky. "Strange," he said.

"The earth has stopped spinning," Neva offered, taking Slew by the hand.

"I knew it was going to be close," Dad said, "and so did Slew. In the last moment, it was taking me in, hiding me within the invisible wall."

I looked into Slew's eye. It was green just like Neva's. It blinked at me and gave me a crooked smile with its thin lips.

"How do you two know each other?" I asked, feeling stupid in an instant. They were obviously from the same planet and had made it out here together. Except – and this I knew for sure – Neva had said nothing about Slew coming along; only that his master had brought him.

"We met here," said Slew. My eyes must have bugged out because Neva reached for my hand. "There are only a few of us left to help you."

Dad smiled. "It seems like forever ago we made the journey here. I'm only sorry that we weren't able to help the Earth in time."

I looked at Dad, really looked at him. He was still wearing the silver suit he'd stolen from the cavern and though it was torn in places, it still held the label on the right sleeve of his uniform: *New American*.

His blue eyes blinked into mine. Mom had her arm around his waist. Tears dripped down her cheeks, slowly traveling down her neck.

"Who were the other men and women at the Green-Eyed Monster?" I asked, for it suddenly occurred to me, how many things I'd gotten wrong –

about Mom, about Dad, about Earth, about Slew and Neva, and who knows what else?

"We are all from the planet Taurus."

"Does the president know?"

Mom laughed. "Of course, she does."

Dad touched his lips. "I'm thirsty," he said. I looked at Dad again. He was about as pale as a picket fence – the ones from the olden days that used to surround people's homes. I'd seen the pictures.

"Over here." I pointed to the spot where I'd managed to fill our now empty jugs.

Dad wiped his hand across his face. "Then, let's go," he said.

The land was a terrible sight this time around, and the sun was beating down on us like there was no tomorrow. Everything, even the fallen trees, were this sickly, white-yellow, and I couldn't feel the air. In its place was an unexplainable void. So, Neva was protecting us from the lack of an atmosphere too.

"We need to get back to civilization," Dad said, taking Mom by the arm. He stumbled a little, causing Mom to fall to the ground. He helped her up and we continued.

I don't know how we made it back to what Dad had mistakenly called "civilization," but we did. I was throwing up by then, and Dad was leaning against the tree, every bit of energy zapped out of him. I turned to Neva.

Neva smiled and turned to my dad.

"Allow me to heal you," it said.

"But we need your power, for the final hour."

"We won't have a final hour if I don't heal you – now," Neva said.

Slew nodded. It was still holding Neva's hand.

I looked at Neva, hoping for an added miracle. None of us would make it; even the trees with their sap would be gone and Slew and Neva wouldn't have food either. The time was now.

Slew looked at me sadly. "Everything is gone. I need sap," it said, looking behind me where the large tree had finally fallen. Everything was hot – dried up.

I wondered if Slew had used its last ounce of power when it had saved my dad from going up in the space plane, but I didn't ask. I thought about it though, all of the people taking Slew's power because they knew they could. They had lived with similar plants before they'd left Taurus to come to Earth. And then another thought struck me.

"Why did we really come here?"

Mom looked at me strangely. "To save the planet."

"But why? Why not stay on Taurus?"

Dad squatted next to me, his blue eyes filling my own. "War."

I thought about all of the wars I'd learned that Earth had gone through, and asked, "So, you ran away from saving *our* planet?"

Mom placed her thin, white hand on my own. "It wasn't like that," she said. "Everyone was warring. Sons and brothers. Mothers and fathers…"

"Even my kind," said Slew. "But we must go. I am feeling weaker by the minute, and we must all eat."

I stood, shaking my bag. "I still have an apple left," I said.

Mom only smiled. "Then, you must save it for later," she answered. "When you're feeling weak."

I couldn't tell Mom that I was feeling weak now, even after the healing from Neva, and that my tongue still felt like an old and crusty branch. But I didn't. I just nodded, and the three of us followed Dad out.

Leaving Ophir Canyon only created more heat and made me even more thirsty. In the valley, the place baked like a human oven, and it wasn't long before my jeans had been torn in favor of shorts, and my shirt removed. I knew I would burn, and even the hat that I'd packed wouldn't shade my face forever. I felt blisters on my skin and wondered what I would look like if I happened upon a mirror.

We sat under the eaves of a building to take in a few breaths. Dad scrounged within it. Six water bottles later, I realized that we'd been resting in front of a grocery store. I placed two of the drinks in my bag, and Mom took the other four for her and Dad.

There was nothing living that I could see, and I felt sorry for Neva and Slew who would be walking a few more miles with us with nothing to eat. We must have looked like a sorrowful group, but no one could see us, being the only beings left living on the planet.

At least that's what I thought that day. That first night away from the Green-Eyed Monster, I actually slept without any terrifying dreams. I dreamt of home, Legos, and our talking plants in the backyard. Funny that I should think of them.

When I awoke, Mom was still asleep, but Dad, Neva, and Slew were just returning from somewhere, cans of food in their hands. No *snap and clip*. But perhaps the thin packaging hadn't made it through the blast. "I don't know why I didn't think of it sooner," Dad said, handing me a can of chili. He had another bag around his shoulders – one he'd managed to get from somewhere – and the thing looked loaded. Slew and Neva had bags of their own, though their complexions were anything but healthy.

They tumbled to the ground when they saw me, and a few cans escaped.

"No trees?" I asked.

"No," Neva answered, its yellow skin reminding me of before. Slew was no better. Even its eye looked tired.

"Have you been walking all night?"

"After you fell asleep, I told Mom what we were planning. She agreed."

Dad was looking better this morning. He'd been healed right after me, and even though his silver suit looked more like a silver swimsuit now, I was grateful for the hands of Neva and the sacrifice it had made for both of us.

The water had done me good the night before, and now food! Dad handed me an old-fashioned can opener. So, they had been in the old school gathering supplies.

I took the silver thing in my hands, and after being told how to work it (Mom had suddenly awakened, and she was eager to share what she'd learned from her grandmother) I opened the tin lid and pulled it off. I dipped my fingers into the warm chili and scooped bits of beans, meat, and juices down my throat, not caring what dripped down my chest. The chili had not obviously been heated by a kitchen burner, but it was still warm.

Mom was handed her own can.

"Protein will be good for all of us, but I've also gathered some canned fruit." Dad smiled over at me as if he'd brought along some ice cream or something. But I didn't complain. As hungry as I was, I'd eaten the apple last night only to still be hungry for more, I was grateful for the canned meal.

I tried not to look at Neva or its companion, for suddenly I knew that they were companions. It just made sense.

It was near the water, about two miles from our sleeping place, that we saw them – men, women, children, a dog. I almost screamed when I saw them, but something about the situation worried me. They weren't moving.

Dad halted my step with his hand.

Neva held a permanent place on my shoulder, and Slew sat wearily on my Dad's shoulder. Neither of them had said anything since the morning meal.

"Youuuuu must be wary," Slew said.

"Listennnnn…" Neva countered.

As we stood, listening, I couldn't hear anything. Not a dog's howl. Not anyone speaking. Not even a whisper through the void above me.

"They are already gone," Mom said, wiping her eyes.

"How do you know?" I asked.

"I can feel them. Only their bodies remain."

I don't know what did it; maybe it was Mom's words, but I realized at that exact moment that my mom had a gift too. She could feel things, things like pain, worry, and death. Perhaps, in her own way, she could read minds like Neva.

"You're right, Aaden," Mom said now, placing her arm around my burned shoulders. Earlier, when she'd noticed what was happening, she'd taken some of my leftover jean material from my bag and wrapped the top of my arms with it; but I could still feel the burn underneath.

"They were picnicking at the time Mercury crashed. While the child and mother were saved in the water, they soon drowned from the heaving of the Earth and lack of an atmosphere."

I felt sick. I touched Mom's hand. "Are we the only ones alive then?" I asked.

I knew in that moment what my mom's answer would be. And it wasn't because I had this marvelous gift of *burning*, but because I had a heart. I hadn't used my heart for more than getting me to and from school, riding on my bike, and stuff like that since I was born, but now I had discovered something else.

"Only those traveling to Mars at the time of impact, and those with plants to help them like Neva and Slew, have survived," she said.

I touched my heart briefly. "So, how did the bear survive?" I asked.

"The bear is probably dead by now," Mom answered.

"How long will we live?" I asked.

"We will not survive indefinitely," Dad said, wiping his forehead as though we were still in the direct heat and Neva was no longer helping us with his protective covering. "We must find the others and leave this place. Where is your compass?"

I reached inside the front pocket and brought the metal piece with the glowing face out.

"See all of the green dots?" Dad asked.

"Yes." There were at least ten of them.

"We need to make our way to the closest one."

I looked down at the compass. "There's another group alive in Utah?" I asked.

"And we should be very grateful that there is," Mom said, placing her hand on my left shoulder where the jean patch was.

We were going to Tooele.

I couldn't believe my dad, but then again, I could. We didn't have a car, and all of the vehicles we'd found at the side of the road wouldn't start. Many of the cars looked more like pancakes anyway. We still ate those, pancakes that is, and I was missing them terribly right now.

Dad said we had a little over nineteen miles to walk. My feet hurt already, and following the road, past the dead and the crushed cars, did little for my sour thoughts. It would take us about two days, Dad said, to get there, not counting the stops we would make, including sleeping, eating and that other unmentionable thing. The good news was that we could do *that* anytime we needed to.

We'd gathered more water on our way out of town – and we each lugged our fair share – excepting Neva and Slew who were too small and much too weak to carry anything but themselves, though most of the time they rode on someone's shoulder. As we walked, the blisters on my feet growing larger, I searched for a tree that stood upright – any tree would do as long as it was green and still in the ground. But I saw nothing.

After a while, I stopped looking and drifted inside myself. No one spoke to me and I didn't speak to them until we stopped for a drink, some food, or to go to the bathroom. By the time evening hit, I was ready for collapse. I sat on the ground, opened a can of chili and began to eat it with my fingers just as I had done that very morning.

Slew and Neva had found some shade under a fallen tree, a tree that looked half dead. There was nothing for them to eat that I could see and I wondered how much longer they would be with us. I knew the dangers of heat exhaustion. I had learned about it in school, still, I wasn't sure how heat exhaustion would apply to two plants not from this world.

I laughed. I wasn't from this world either.

"A joke?" Dad asked, making me laugh some more. I choked on a bean and swallowed the warm water.

"No joke. Do you think we're going to make it?"

Mom lifted her head from her bag that was currently serving as her pillow and reached for the canned pears. Reaching her fingers in, she took a bite. "I'm thankful for this," she said. "And I think we're going to make it."

It was night again, although the sun still beat down on us, and I figured for the first time, that those on the other side of the planet would be complaining too – of being too cold, and not seeing the sun anymore. I wondered what that would be like, but I didn't wonder for long. The next time I opened my eyes, Dad was handing me a can of peaches.

"Eat quickly, we have a long day ahead," he said.

I ate and checked on Neva and Slew – both of them were solid white.

I looked over at Mom and her look said everything. It wouldn't be long now.

The Journey

I don't know if I should tell you this, but by the time we'd found a living tree – we were already through about a day of walking by then – I wondered if my two new friends were dead.

Dad pointed at the tree, still standing upright, or at least, semi-upright, next to what looked like water. I was so thirsty I couldn't stand it. I ran.

Once I'd reached the pool, I drank all I could and refilled my jug. I could feel Mom and Dad beside me. Only then did I think to reach for Neva. The plant was no longer on my shoulder.

Slew was still on my Dad's shoulder, and he placed it on the ground next to the water and practically jumped on the tree. Taking a knife from his bag he slit the trunk to look inside. "I think we may have a winner here!" he said, looking at me. "Where's Neva?"

"I don't know!" I cried, searching around me.

"Help me with Slew!" Dad screamed. I raced to the spot where Slew had been placed, picked it up and raced to the side of my dad.

"Open its mouth!"

I opened Slew's mouth but saw nothing but darkness. Its flesh was a ghostly white, almost see through. Dad placed semi-dry pieces of sap inside Slew's mouth. Slew's eyes were closed and I couldn't feel a pulse or anything.

The stuff must have been sticky, and I hoped it would dissolve easily into Slew's mouth.

Suddenly, Mom was beside me. "Here! I need some too!" she said, reaching for Dad's knife.

"Wait, I'll do it."

I turned to see Mom holding Neva across her lap like a newborn baby. Neva's eye was closed, and its thin lips were black. I couldn't believe it.

In moments, I was helping Dad and then Mom with the mouths of both Slew and Neva. I am not sure how long we worked at this healing balm, but it was long enough to make my arms ache. Still, when Slew finally opened its eye, and it stared at me, unblinking, I felt like there was some hope. Moments later, Neva's eye opened, and I was reminded of the green glow within the cave and the power I had obtained. Still, I didn't hold the healing power, and I supposed I never would. I could barely handle walking through rock.

It was the morning of the second day before Neva spoke. It needed help sitting up, and then it reached for me. I took its yellow hand and apologized for running.

But Neva had no recollection of me running and so I was suddenly grateful for that. Slew, on the other hand, looked over at me wearily and with such strong intent, I wondered if it had seen something Neva hadn't.

"We have a good day's walk left," Dad began, unzipping his bag. "This is all that's left," he added, handing me a can of corn and Mom a can of green beans.

I was about to ask what Dad was eating when he closed his bag and looked up the street. There were cars everywhere on the freeway – dead people too, and animals of varying sizes – including animals that should have been further up in the canyon. But even they must have been looking for food.

I thought briefly about the bear and our narrow escape and wondered what Dad would think when I told him all Mom and me had gone through. But there wasn't time for that now.

We took shelter as often as we could, but my skin was more than likely burned to a crisp though I'd decided to put my shirt back on – such as it was. Mom's face was red, and Dad's matched it. We must have looked something like bacon.

Interestingly, I felt heavier somehow, and there were times I wondered if I was gaining weight instead of losing it with all of the walking and the blasted heat.

There were fires now everywhere I looked, and as we got closer to our destination, it was all I could do to remain positive.

What would we really find when we got to the city? Would the others still be there as Dad had promised? And if so, what would we do then? We couldn't live on this planet the way it was.

I looked down at the compass and watched the blinking green dot that would turn blue when we were much closer to our destination. I thought about my friend, Bronty. Thought about his trip not really being a trip away from Earth. I thought about all of the times I'd started those fires, not really knowing that I had started them. I thought about a lot of things as we walked, as a family, to Tooele. But it wasn't until I saw the woman, that I began to have real hope.

She looked like an angel.

"Who are you?" she asked first.

The woman wore a silver suit, and her hair was black. Spreading the fine strands with her long fingers, she peered up at us, as if we were not really there, but ghosts ourselves.

"I am Jachin, a *New American*. And this is my wife, Fonda, and my son, Aaden."

"And these two?"

"Neva and Slew."

The woman smiled. "I am Barina. Welcome to Space Doc 5."

Green Light

I looked down at the compass. The dot was still green.

"We have to take precautions," said the woman known as Barina. "In the beginning, there were far too many trying to find a way off the planet. We wanted to help them, of course, but without a monophyla, they were beyond hope."

"A what?" I asked.

"Let's get out of the hot sun first," said Barina, walking ahead, and leading us up the road. I couldn't see anything. And then it came to me. What was there was invisible. "You can be sure we're happy to see you," Barina continued, leading us along.

When we stopped we weren't alone; there were at least half a dozen humans and at least one monophyla in the same place as the space plane, standing out in the open. They were all wearing silver suits. I didn't recognize any of them, but Dad did.

He reached out his hand to one of them, a man with a beard – quite a bit taller than me. His beard was white.

"I hardly recognized you," Dad said.

The man pulled Dad into a tight hug. He was smaller than my dad but not by much. "I can't believe it!"

"Neither can I, actually. I thought you were…"

"For a time, but when things got bad…"

Dad smiled and turned to Mom. "This is my wife, Fonda, and my son…"

"So, this is Aaden," the man said, leaving my dad and walking over to me. The entire place, other than the plane, was a barrage of broken metal, cracked tree limbs, and unrecognizable garbage. "I'm glad to finally meet you." He held out his hand. "I'm… George."

"George?"

I took George's hand. He was wearing silver gloves.

"Can't be too careful, even here," George said, turning to my mom and grinning over at her. "Let's get into some shade."

I followed George as he led us beyond the space plane and to a pile of tree limbs stacked on top of one another. There was a shady place inside, though I wondered how those at Space Doc 5 had managed to get everything stacked without equipment.

"There are many gifts," Mom said as if reading my thoughts.

I sat on the ground. Dad followed and then Mom. Neva was once again on my shoulder; Slew, the shoulder of my dad.

George stood in front of us. "Now that you're here," he began, "we may finally have enough monophyla to get this craft off the ground."

I watched as the others – three men and one woman – entered the safety of the shade and sat down behind him.

"The power is almost gone here. Even with the monophyla…" George paused and looked behind him. "It has done all it can. How are your two?"

Dad shook his head. "Still healing, I'm afraid. They will be of little help."

George caressed his beard. It had clumps of dried dirt in it, and his face looked like leather. "Still, we need to try. All of our food is gone."

"How long?"

"Two days now."

"And water?"

"We finished the last jug this morning."

Dad turned to me and nodded. I couldn't believe it. He wanted me to give George the only food I had? I looked over at Mom, and then I felt something against my shoulder. Neva dropped to the ground and stood before me. One green eye blinked up. At that moment, I noticed Neva's skin had returned to its natural color.

I looked at Slew, trying to avoid my dad's hardened gaze. Slew's skin was also green.

"Okay," I said, reaching in my bag. I heard Mom doing the same.

With the can of green beans and the additional can of corn before us, I reached for the can opener.

"Wait!" George said, stopping my hand. There was a rush of words from behind him. He motioned the other humans over. They sat near him like children, their voices quiet.

I don't know if you're going to understand this, but once I got my can open, and Mom had her can open, the silver gloves were suddenly off of everybody's hands, and we were taking turns reaching in. The cans were passed around like communion at a Catholic Mass, but instead of giving we were all taking.

Two reaches later, both cans were empty.

"Thank you," the woman in silver said. I looked closer. Really close. The woman had the same dark hair as another woman I had met, and though her skin was red from the heat of the sun, her eyes were blue, the color of water. It couldn't be her, could it?

In the next instant, I knew.

"You!" I shrieked, standing. I reached for her middle. Pushing her to the ground I found her face. I don't know how many times I hit her before Dad pulled me away.

I shrieked in his arms then – shrieked like a girl – but I didn't care. This was the woman, the same woman who had not let us on board the space plane; the same woman who had forced Slew into taking my parents' memories away. The same one who had told us to go to the shelter! And she was not only alive but here!

"I thought you'd be in Taurus by now." I tried to spit. But my mouth was dry and I couldn't.

The woman stood and brushed herself off – as if that mattered. She blinked over at me, her blue eyes shadowed by matted black hair.

"We didn't make it as you can see."

It was then I vaguely recognized everyone except for George. I looked over at the space plane – *our* space plane. It looked damaged, but I could see some repair work had been done.

"Some of its passengers died upon impact," George said. "And with the shuttle not in working order, we have been waiting for you."

Now I was terrified. "Me? Why?"

"You have the power to get us out of here."

I thought about how I'd saved my dad and Slew from the thick walls of Ophir Canyon with the power of the green stone, and wondered if the old man meant that. And if they did, they probably knew all about it.

I felt a hand on my shoulder. "Yes, he has it," Mom said.

I stood silently, taking the words in. Sure, I had the stone, but they couldn't have it. If the stone could take us to the Rentaurus System and to the planet,

Taurus, then my family and I would go. We would leave them here just like they'd planned on leaving us.

Mom must have sensed my feelings because she took me in her arms. "Give us a moment?" she asked.

Turning from the group, she led me further into the shelter. Dad followed, carrying Slew on his shoulder. I wasn't sure where Neva was. Reaching for its leg my hand came away empty.

"I don't get it."

"Listen, son. They didn't know you had it. Well, not until recently." He looked over at Mom.

"You mean, Mom has a power, too?"

"Of course I do. But you have the greatest power."

The words pricked up my legs like a moving chill.

"Mom?"

Mom took my hand. "You are the fulfilling of prophecy."

"The…"

"Prophecy, Aaden. In our world, a story is told of one young and with power that would save us. When our planet grew in hatred, your father and I wondered how you could possibly save it. You were just a child. We came here, hoping to protect you, hoping that in time we would know what it was that you were to do."

"Me?"

Mom smiled. "The fires, remember? You had the power to burn, and if the power to burn, the power to retrieve the stone, and the power to get us home."

I couldn't believe it, or could I? "But, we don't have a home to return to."

"Not a home on Taurus," Slew said next to my ear. "But with the green stone we can travel far, and no one has to get old, no one has to die."

"Why all of the secrets? I mean, why didn't you tell me all of this stuff before?"

Mom smiled. "I wasn't sure it was you at first, and besides, son, you weren't ready, and I'm afraid you're not ready now."

"Sure, I am! We will leave the silver suits here, all of them, excepting maybe George, he's nice. And we will take the stone and I will do whatever it takes to get us out of here."

Slew blinked its eye. I could see terror there.

"What?" I shouted. "What!?"

"Remember what you've learned." Dad peered down at me and smiled, but I didn't get it. Even Slew smiled crookedly, but I still didn't get it.

If you're thinking right now that yes, Aaden is about the densest person on the planet, you're probably right. Almost everyone was dead anyway, so that would, of course, make me an easy target. I was frankly – mad, okay? I didn't see how calming myself down would make any difference. We would just enter the space plane, I would take the stone inside, and all would be well. We would take off and leave this miserable planet behind us along with everyone else miserable that was left on it.

"Faith, you must have faith," Neva said.

I turned and stared down at the little plant that had become my best friend. Bronty was gone, would forever be gone, but I still had Neva.

"Faith precedes the miracle," I said flatly.

"That's right."

"Well, I guess I'll never be humble enough to have faith," I said.

Neva blinked and hopped on my shoulder.

"It's time," It said, "For you to know the truth."

"What truth?"

Suddenly, George stood beside me. "I agree," he said.

Freedom?

Do you know what freedom looks like?

I didn't until that moment. What looked to me like an old man, a man intent on getting the other silver wearers off this planet, was, in fact, someone I knew.

"We didn't get to Mars," George said.

"I know, you crashed."

"That's right, but something happened."

"What?"

George looked deeply into my eyes as if he was going to kiss me – only he didn't. He just stared and kept staring. When I screamed, he punched me in the arm.

"Bronty?" I gasped.

The old man – my friend – nodded.

I couldn't believe it, I couldn't believe my eyes.

An old man stood before me, a really old man, with wrinkled skin and a slouching posture. But the eyes, they were the same as I remembered them.

"Where are your parents?" I asked.

"Gone."

"I'm sorry."

"Don't be. It was a sacrifice traveling back. Watching Mercury crash into the Earth. Mars showering rock. Getting old long before I should have."

"How?" I asked.

"We tried to speed things up; it was an experiment. Instead of fifty years, it was days before we came within the Rentaurus System. But there was no one there to help. They were all dead because of war. We made our journey back – we had only hours instead of years to get here – and by the time we reached the Earth's atmosphere, Mars was breaking up. The shuttle crashed. I brought advancements back with me. Only, when we returned, it was too late."

My friend looked down at his old and wrinkly hands. "The aging process as you know it, is different in space without gravity. Everything – muscles, bone, skin, is fast-forwarded. If the space plane is going faster than its purpose, quick aging occurs."

"But my parents didn't have a problem coming here when I was little," I said.

"What took them five years, took me just a few hours," said Bronty. "The planes can travel that fast, but it isn't always in our best interest to go as fast as we can."

George peered over at me. I couldn't tell if he was smiling or frowning, his beard was as thick as a bush around his face. But I could see Bronty in his eyes. It occurred to me that my dad had known Bronty the moment he had seen him even though the man had introduced himself as George, but I shrugged the thought aside, if only for a moment, so I could learn how Bronty thought he was going to save the planet.

"We didn't know it was you, of course, at least not at first. Though we'd tried for the previous few years to scavenge the green rock crystal from Ophir Canyon, we'd always come away empty-handed. All of us had tools – even drills. And we had invisibility. Healing. Mind reading. We thought we could walk within the rock, heal the rock, find out what the rock was thinking and do what we needed to do to bring the green stones to the surface, but nothing worked. We helped build sky planes until I thought we were all going to go crazy, hoping and praying, that we would still be able to save the planet. But it was no use. In my father's day, he wasn't believed – species like Neva and Slew continued to be treated as slaves, and by the time my father was believed, we couldn't work fast enough – without the stone."

Bronty's words as an old man were almost too much to take in. And then Mom spoke.

"My gift told me that you were a special boy, but I had my own doubts for years. During our capture, I had some time to think about things, and I wondered if your power was the answer we'd been looking for."

"Am I the only one?" I asked.

"Yes." Mom held me close.

It took some doing, but my heart began to soften after that. The astronauts, the ones who had taken off initially without us, and had crashed to the Earth, needed a second chance. In the real fear of dying, they had perhaps done the only thing they knew to do – save themselves.

It was a selfish act, I knew that just like I knew I was selfish and had been selfish since the day I was born. It took a lot for me to see clearly enough to think outside myself, but I knew I had to do it. My friend, Bronty, hadn't known about his father's secret mission, even on that last day he'd said goodbye to me, telling me he was traveling to Mars because his father was an engineer. He hadn't known then what he would be called to do. And yet, he had done it, getting old in the process.

How could I do any less?

Bronty would always be my friend. He was old, sure, but that same light that I had always known about him still flickered from his eyes. It was like a sliver of light had found its way through the crack of the cave wall and was now shining within the damaged hull of the space plane. Sure, the space plane was banged up, the shuttle, scarred; if alive, they would have both been dead. But one of them would rise and take us away from this place – just a floating chunk of rock now.

167

I wasn't sure where we'd travel next. I wasn't even sure if we'd make it. But we wouldn't give up. I knew that. As I looked into the eyes of my 'old' friend I knew he knew it too. With our gifts, the stone, and each other, we just had to make it.

"So, the space plane, does it work?"

"Yes, and with your help, there will finally be enough lift." George smiled and punched me in the arm again.

I thought about my friend's last words as he sat down to rest in the home we would live in for who knows how long.

"You don't need to worry about getting old," he said. "If it takes five years, fifty, or more, your parents won't age, and neither will you."

When I looked up at him, amazed, the old man only smiled. "Remember when you were protected after Mercury hit the Earth? Remember when Mars scattered all around you, and you still remained standing?"

"*That* was hard to forget," I told him.

"That protective barrier is the very essence of monophyla. How do you think plants weathered all of the harsh Earth winters? How do you think they made it through the heat of summer? Aaden, you will never age. Never."

"Never?" I asked.

In seconds, the stone was out of my bag and, as the bright green light filtered through the cracks of the space plane, I listened as the engine purred and the plane lifted from Earth for the last time.

I am Aaden Prescott

If you've read this far, you know what has happened to Earth, who I really am, and that I'm traveling on a space plane. Though there are things I'm not prepared to tell you, at least not yet, there are things I think you should know – especially since you've obviously found me sometime in the future.

Maybe you're doing a history project, maybe you just like to learn about people who lived long ago; in either case, I'm glad you've followed me this far.

Once we'd cleared Earth, I almost didn't look out the window. When I did, my heart did something funny, as if it wanted to stop or something. I stared out. All of us did, at the chunk of rock, we'd once known as Earth.

The Earth had a big hole in the side of it, sort of like a ragged bite, and it was no longer blue and green – more like a pasty yellow and white.

Neva sat on my shoulder and tried to take my mind off of it.

He told me about the plants in the Rentaurus System, and why they'd never received names. Having advanced from the 'under the ground' variety, they grew, only to be used and discarded at their masters' choice. My naming of Neva was the first time a plant had ever been named that had two legs. Before me, all plants were considered lower than pets, and it was on the planet Taurus, that things had begun to get out of hand, and monophyla's had begun to escape.

As we flew farther from Earth, when it was only a tiny speck in the vast sky, Slew, whom I'd just named Stella for star, spoke about the once kind society that had turned through the millennia. What had once been considered sacred – the bearing of gifts – had become ordinary, and something to use against others.

It was not only the planet Earth but people and aliens who turned light shade, she said.

She had been afraid, said she was still afraid until she'd met Neva, her companion.

Watching the window, I could no longer see Earth and the loss of it frightened me. Where would we go now? How many years would we travel before we reached our destination? If Taurus was fifty years away, how many more years would we have to travel before we found somewhere to plant our feet?

Even if it took more than fifty years to get to a habitable planet, I knew I wouldn't age. We all had the protection of the monophyla to combat that. Still, we might be wandering the skies for eons with nowhere to plant our feet.

And that was something I hardly wanted to think about.

Stella's sacrifice, her lie about wiping out my memories, had allowed my family and I to escape the caves, and ultimately to leave planet Earth, but – for what?